CAGE OF ROOTS

MATT GRIFFIN

THE O'BRIEN PRESS
DUBLIN

First published 2015 by The O'Brien Press Ltd,
12 Terenure Road East, Rathgar, Dublin 6, Ireland.
Tel: +353 1 4923333; Fax: +353 1 4922777
E-mail: books@obrien.ie
Website: www.obrien.ie

ISBN: 978-1-84717-681-3

10 9 8 7 6 5 4 3 2 1
20 19 18 17 16 15

Cover image: Matt Griffin
Printed and bound by CPI Group (UK) Ltd, Croydon, CR0 4YY
The paper in this book is produced using pulp from managed forests.

The O'Brien Press receives financial assistance from

For my girls

ACKNOWLEDGEMENTS

I would like to thank Michael O'Brien, Emma Byrne, Susan Houlden and all at the O'Brien Press for taking a punt on me; my parents, brothers, sisters-in-law and friends for their constant encouragement and, most of all, my wife, Orla, for her endless faith and patience.

Contents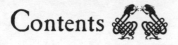

Chapter 1 - A Lingering Nightmare   page 10

Chapter 2 - An Empty Bed   19

Chapter 3 - A Stifling Cell   40

Chapter 4 - An Audience with Ancients   55

Chapter 5 - A Spiralling Path   72

Chapter 6 - A Bright Light in the Deep Earth   86

Chapter 7 - A Door in Time   101

Chapter 8 - A Map Misread   123

Chapter 9 - A Weave of Roots   144

Chapter 10 - A Test for Treasure   160

Chapter 11 - A Secret's Bite   185

Chapter 12 - A Battle Below   208

Chapter 13 - A Song of Goodbye   224

CHAPTER 1

A Lingering Nightmare

Ayla was having a nightmare. The most vivid, horrifying nightmare.

She woke because she could not breathe. She was in stifling, hot darkness; like when you fall asleep with the heat on but a hundred times worse. What little air there was tasted of mud, and the darkness was absolute. Her room was never this dark. She couldn't even see her hand in front of her face.

There was something else too that made her realise this wasn't her own room. She could sense the closeness of the walls. Even though she couldn't see, she knew that where she was lying was small and tight; when she reached out her fingers she found the walls around her all too quickly. Her nails scratched at hardened muck, and the dust hissed as it fell from her touch to the rough, cragged floor. She started to grope blindly and frantically, and tried to stand too quickly, banging her head painfully on the low ceiling. She could only hunch. A tremor of panic grew deep in her stomach as she searched for an opening but found none. She covered every centimetre again and again, finding that she could move just less than a metre on either side and never stand to her full height. The desperate search sucked the adrenaline from her and she stopped, spent, and lay against one of the walls.

So, she decided, she was in the middle of the worst nightmare she had ever had: a horribly realistic, graphic one of being buried alive. All she had to do was clench her eyes shut, as tight as she could, and go back to sleep. But sleep just wouldn't arrive, and she couldn't escape the feeling that she was just about to run out of air. It was so uncomfortable, and the hard, knotty ground she lay on was just too real. As Ayla slowly accepted her situation as fact, her screams for help morphed to sobs in the blackness.

She felt that there was no sense of time in this waking grave, but it seemed like she had been crying for hours. Her throat was raw from shouting for help, and her chest ached from heaving. Her hands and feet hurt too, from kicking and lashing at the walls.

When she accepted defeat at last, and lay jolting with those sharp breaths you can't help but make after crying, rational Ayla began to wake. She told herself: *lying here sobbing is going to get me nowhere.* Punching walls of muck and stone wasn't particularly helpful either. She had to think – to cast her mind back to every single minute of the day and try to guess how she had come to be buried alive. Did she fall? Ayla loved to walk in the woods. Maybe she had tripped into a ditch or badger hole and the memory of it was knocked out of her? She did her best to calm herself and recall the steps of her day, starting with a rushed breakfast with her beloved uncles.

Breakfasts were always eaten in panic, because Ayla always overslept. Every school day played out the same way too: Uncle Lann, cross and rushing her; Uncle Taig, tutting sarcastically and winking; and Uncle Fergus, himself a sleeper, dropping off again at the table. Thinking of her uncles helped ease the worst of the terror. She indulged the memories, lingering in their warmth.

They were her only family. The day they rescued her was still so clear four years later: they pulled her from the torment of St Sophia's Holy Home for Girls in New York State. Before that day she did not even know she had any family at all, let alone that they, and therefore she, were as Irish as spuds. Lann, Fergus and Taig were giants of men, each as tall as two-and-a-half metres. When she was called out of the blue to the cold visitors' room, they were there, stooping under the ceiling. Straight away they sent beaming smiles Ayla's way and she would never forget the look of defeat in the sisters' cruel faces. She would have leapt into a tiger's arms to get away from those nuns, but three hulking goliaths from an island she had barely heard of? It was nearly a more frightening prospect. It took more visits, and a lot of talk, before she would trust them. In the end, it came down to a simple choice: stay incarcerated with the sisters, or leave for a new adventure in Ireland. The day they drove away and St Sophia's faded into the distance was still the most magical of her life. The long flight over the Atlantic was a rebirth, plain and simple, from despair to hope.

Underground Ayla bit her lip and focused. *This morning was no different than any other,* she thought. *Breakfast was only half-eaten. I ran out the door with toast hanging from my mouth, and we sped off in that dirty old jeep. Fergus's snoring was louder than the engine, like always. And I was dropped at the school gates with only a minute to spare before the bell, like always.*

It was so hard to get comfortable in the blackness, thinking back got more difficult with every minute. Even warm thoughts of saying farewell to St Sophia's were no match for the rocks and twigs that were now knuckling into her back. But sharpening her thoughts was essential; piecing together the day should, must, reveal some clues as to how she got here and how she could get out. So Ayla calmed herself again, sucked in a sip of stale air, and brought her mind back to the morning, and the first hours of school.

She had just avoided Mrs Marnagh, the principal, and made it to her first class before everyone had settled in their desks. Sean and Benvy sat tapping their watches and grinning, by now a morning ritual. She threw her eyes to heaven, smiled, and took her seat at the opposite end of the classroom. Ayla had long been separated from them because of their fondness for talking, laughing and distracting each other as much as possible.

That morning, Irish was their first class: a favourite. While there was no joy for her in history or geography, Irish was something she was good at. It just came naturally to her, albeit with a mild New York twang, and it helped that her uncles insisted on speaking it to her at home. That morning, she remembered, Mr O'Ceallaigh was writing on the whiteboard, but she was engrossed with something outside. She noticed a harmless movement in the bank of trees across the pitches: just wind making the leaves dance. But it looked so strange. The leaves made lithe shadows that scurried like a troop of skinny baboons, leaping through the branches. They were so realistic she had laughed out loud.

She rubbed her eyes and opened them to find that Mr O'Ceallaigh had stopped writing and was staring at her. She was sorry because she liked him, but allowed herself one more glance to confirm that leaves were just leaves and wind was just wind and her head was just having fun with her, as it so often did. The trees swung, fanned by the late autumn breeze – and there was no sign of any baboons leaping through the branches!

The rest of the day, as far as she could remember, went by without incident. She strained to think of anything out of the ordinary, but nothing really of note had happened. It was Wednesday, and that meant finishing off with the Seventh Hell of double-maths. Double-maths always seemed like a time-stretching purgatory of dullness, where even clocks seemed to fall asleep, and Mr Fenlon's voice became like the drone note on Taig's uilleann pipes. At last, after an age spent confused by Xs and Ys, the bell went and it was time for home.

Now Ayla really had to concentrate because, despite her best efforts, the memories from this part of the day seemed to dance around like moths, impossible to hold. She squirmed on the rugged floor, stamped her feet in frustration, and had another bout of tears. But this was Emotional Ayla fighting for dominance, and she forced Rational Ayla back into the driving seat. 'Calm, Ayla,' she said aloud, and repeated the words until the sobbing stopped.

She had messed around with Sean and Benvy at the wall beside the parking area. They were jostling about, play-fighting: a blessed relief from maths-boredom. Sean was playing 'Poke the Tiger' with Benvy, holding his finger just a few centimetres from her face. Benvy, at nearly twice Sean's size and with a fuse a tenth as long, was an easy target. Ayla was distracted by the noise of the wind in the leaves. It seemed so loud. Like every single leaf was shouting at her. She was snapped out of it when Sean knocked her over onto the grass, launched by an angry Benvy. He had committed the mortal sin of teasing her about her size – the one thing she could never stand – and Sean was punished accordingly. *We were all laughing about it, though. They got on their bus and I walked. Just a normal day.*

Was this when I went to the woods? She often took a detour through Coleman's Woods, as it edged onto the back of her house. She loved those cool minutes in the whispering green trees. It gave her time alone to let her mind drift. In her own company she was never the 'different one'. Ayla the Yankee. Ayla the orphan. Ayla the big fellas' niece. She was just Ayla. But she had not taken that route this time. She remembered now, she had felt so *tired*. Not just sleepy but … weary. Spent, even. It was such a strange feeling. *So this isn't a badgers' set or a dark ditch, and I haven't just slipped in the woods and hit my head.* That was not good news, for there went the most plausible and normal explanation. All that was left was fear.

At least she knew now that this option was off the cards. She could move on in her memories to the next step: the walk home. And, yes, here things became clearer, briefly.

The walk through her hometown of Kilnabracka took her away from Main Street to John's Lane and past Daly's sweet shop, but she didn't go in, for once. Up on Synge Hill, she walked past the rows of tiny bungalows where old ladies lived, but were never seen. It brought her down to Lee's Valley Road, where her estate, Rathlevean, and two other estates her uncles built, edged up the next hill. She was too tired to notice the wind had picked up in the branches of Coleman's Woods, beyond the houses. She went straight over to her road, trudging now and dragging her feet with fatigue. She lifted the key to the door, shaking off a momentary relapse into her 'monkey' daydream when the wind made funny shapes resembling baboons in the big sycamore leaves. She threw her bag under the stairs, and on her way up to her room decided to ignore a text from Finny, and just collapse into bed. The memory stopped before her head was halfway to the pillow.

A spark ignited: a flash of a thought. Her stomach fluttered at the prospect. My phone! Frantically, desperately, she fumbled about her pockets, patting herself down, cursing at every empty pocket until – there in her back pocket! What she had mistaken for a rock or branch digging into her was her phone. Sobbing again, this time with relief, she pulled it out and pressed the button. The screen lit up. But almost as quickly, just long enough to see there was no signal, the device beeped once and slipped into darkness, along with her hope.

Ayla just lay there then, staring into nothing. Time loped along half-dead again, until from something (her phone? No, it was the wrong kind of glow) light appeared again. A chink of orange in the blackness by her feet, and it grew. Struggling to sit up and not knowing whether to laugh, cry, scream or sing, she watched the glow spread, and the chink widen. But instead of some friendly Garda's hand, or, please God, a great hairy ham of an uncle's paw, something totally different blocked the light. It froze her blood.

Obstructing the glow, suddenly, was a head, but such a strange one – a horrible one: black with two bulbous, glowing white eyes. Ears darted out either side like wrecked kitchen knives, and the mouth? When it opened, it was like looking into a furnace, burning red, stinging her eyes. And it spoke, or made a sound anyway. A sound like metal dragged on stone, and a long, thin, twisted claw of a hand reached in to drop something at her feet, something that smelled of rotting leaves, and withdrew. The hole snapped shut, and Ayla was left again in pitch, hot blackness, too stunned to cry.

CHAPTER 2

An Empty Bed

As another freezing bluster of hail threw itself against him, Fergus hoisted a pile of blocks onto the first bay of scaffold. He didn't need a ladder. Huge, mountainous Fergus, with pond-green eyes and a bulbous nose set in a bracken of red hair and orange beard. His hands alone were the size of a normal man's chest, and he delighted anyone who asked with feats of strength. But this was work-time, and great Fergus was hard at it, over-enthusiastically, as was his way.

There was a famous photo over the turf fire in Greely's of Fergus holding a bunch of patrons aloft, three on each arm, while balancing a pint of stout on his head. In this photo, which was the pride of the pub (although no one seemed to remember when it was taken), Fergus's two brothers can be seen behind him: Taig, fairer than him, and smaller too, although himself well over two-and-a-half metres and

a hundred and fifty-odd kilos, laughing his blond head off, and Lann, the eldest, scowling at yet more foolishness from his brother. The picture summed them up pretty well.

Fergus was a behemoth, who loved all the attention he could muster. He was always the loudest voice in Greely's, the core of the craic. His voice was like a storm in summer, a low boom crackling with drama, so the hairs on your neck would stand up when he spoke, and yet it was full of warmth.

Taig was the musician: expert at the bodhrán, guitar, uilleann pipes and whistle, he could get any foot in the world tapping, and silence it in the next minute with an old air of breathtaking beauty. He was like Fergus in that he loved laughter, and whenever the big man was making a scene, you could be sure Taig would be in stitches beside him.

Lann was different. It wasn't that he was grim, just that he always seemed like he had serious matters on his mind and no room left for joking. He was renowned as a fair man, a good employer of anyone with decent skill in building, and if you had him build you a house you'd never have to move for the rest of your life. But he was not entirely merry, that was for sure.

Lann's brow was a ploughed field lined with furrows. His thick, black eyebrows sheltered iron-coloured eyes, which sat deep in his face, ever watchful. They could bore through a man at fifty metres; the lads on the site often joked that he could shoot lasers out of them! But alas, that wasn't true. His dark mane was long and tied at the back, his nose and mouth set into his square face like they were carved out of stone. Like Taig, he kept the whiskers off his chin, but his angular jaw was curtained by dense sideburns. He stood just over two metres, with wide shoulders to carry whatever burden it was that kept his mood so serious. He was fearsome to see, for sure. But anyone who knew him knew he was fair, honest and good, and they didn't fear him unless they were late for work more than once. Like the other two, you wouldn't be able to guess his age. They all looked young and old at the same time, and in fact it was a common game to guess their age in Greely's, but the big fellas never told.

The wind was whipping sleet from the west onto the men who worked on the build. It was a big renovation job: Sheedys', an old farmhouse that sat nestled in thick oak and birch at the foot of some small hillocks near Knock-white Hill, about five kilometres out of town in the area of Dundearg. A couple from Limerick had bought the old place from Pat Sheedy and they had big changes in store. A new extension built here, outhouses transformed there. If you were lucky on a day like this you were a carpenter or electrician, working inside on the first fix. For the bricklayers outside, it was less pleasant, especially for Tom Skellig, whose toes were nearly crushed by another row of blocks dumped at his feet by over-zealous Fergus.

'Mind Tom's feet, for God's sake, Fergus!' Lann shouted, as the red giant hoisted yet another row of seven blocks onto the scaffold and slammed them down to be met, as Lann had expected, with a holler from poor Tom.

'Ah, Jaysus, Fergus!' Tom squealed, clutching his foot and trying to get the boot off. 'Even with steel-toed boots I'm not safe!'

He got the mangled boot off and began to blow on his foot.

'Ah, did Poor Possum hurt his little toe-toes?' Fergus chided, while laughter trickled down from Taig, skipping between the higher levels of scaffold.

Lann brought his fist down on the plans in frustration. He had been using a pile of blocks as a table. Several of them cracked.

'Stop!' yelled Lann, with a keen edge of anger in his voice. It was a rare baring of teeth from the oldest brother, and it was enough to quieten the whole site, including his brothers.

'Sorry, Lann,' said Fergus, and he gently lifted just a couple of blocks onto the platform, well away from Tom.

Lann frowned down upon the now-torn plans. He knew it was unusual for him to be so quick to temper.

Sure, the architect was proving to be a bit of a pain in his neck – a posh fella from Dublin, and prone to change his plans – but something else was agitating him, and what it was he couldn't say or put his finger on. He just had an ill feeling about the day, and this was a feeling he had learned not to ignore over the years. For now though, he just couldn't nail it down.

He took out his phone and looked at the photo of Ayla, for the picture always calmed him. He stared into the green eyes, glimmering between the masses of amber curls, and checked himself for losing his temper. He knew Ayla would disapprove if she were there. 'Sorry pet,' he muttered, and put the phone back in his pocket. Before he could return to the plans, he heard a polite cough behind him.

Mr Fitzgerald, the architect, stood beside him wearing all the gear: hard hat with built-in ear-guards and visor, hi-viz jacket, vest and pants, and brand new boots without a single scuff. Behind him were the couple that had bought the house; all three held umbrellas pointlessly against the sleet. The wind swept up and under and from the side, and paid no heed to brollies.

Lann barely noticed the rain bouncing off his face. This was a scheduled visit; he had just uncharacteristically forgotten about it. It was the last thing he needed today.

'What can I do for you, Mr Fitzgerald?' he asked.

'Hello Lann. How's it going? Horrible day so it is,' the

architect replied in his tangy South-Dublin drawl.

'Soft enough alright,' replied Lann, as the icy wind broke another wave of hail against his cheek.

'Well, you'll remember I let you know we would be coming by to discuss a few adjustments. We have a small change or two anyway.'

The changes were anything but small, and the architect's voice seemed to shake with pride at his own visionary abilities.

'It's all been approved at the planners. Here's the USB with the new plans, and of course a printed copy – we know you don't like computers!' he finished with a smile. The couple attempted to grin expectantly behind him, but they just ended up wincing against the pelting wet.

Briefly, Lann considered shouting at all of them, but withheld his frustration and simply announced to the site: 'Tom! Stop. Fergus, take the blocks down. Taig! Put that scaffold back up!' He turned to the three visitors. 'No worries.'

Mr Fitzgerald smiled, satisfied his power over such a giant had not waned. 'Good man, Lann. Now, we also wanted to look into the structure in the northeast corner, the little rocky hillock. We talked about this bef—'

But before he could finish, Lann held up a great slab of hand.

'That'll be all for now, Mr Fitzgerald. We've enough to be getting on with.'

'But, eh, Lann, we've been wanting to talk about this before and …'

Lann had returned to his desk of grey blocks, turning his back to the three drowned visitors.

'We'll talk about it again. We have a lot to be doing. Mr and Mrs Moran, feel free to head on in to the main house and take a look around, but take a hat from the office first and no going into the extension. We'll be taking half of it down now.'

There was a tone in his voice that said 'This is not up for negotiation', and the three headed to the prefab office to fetch another couple of hard hats. Lann muttered under his breath, crumpled the torn plans into a ball, and sighed, casting his iron eyes to the stony hillock in the northeast corner.

Finny's knees ached from kneeling on the hardwood floor. He was only about a tenth of the way through the 'S's' in the old phone book, and already he had been there for at least an hour and a half. Writing out a letter of Fr Shanlon's 1993 Telecom Éireann phone book was the lanky priest's favourite penance, and Finny seemed to have to do it every second day. He wouldn't mind, but it wasn't even for doing anything bad. In his school, the slightest step out of line meant big punishment. But big punishment was fine by him, and the more they gave out to him, the harder he pushed back.

It wasn't so much that he loved to cause trouble – it was more that he hated being told what to do, especially by grown-ups. He had no faith in their authority, let alone any respect for it, and it made him angry whenever he thought about how they tried to control him, to push and pull and tug at him, constantly. He just wanted to be left alone, to hang out with his friends who never tried to direct or persuade him. Ayla, especially, just let him be.

He did miss the hurling; that part stung. But it was the same out there on the pitch – they just wouldn't let him express himself. *Run here, mark him, you should be here,* they would shout, and he would shut them up with a point from halfway. They hit him where it hurt now anyway – no hurling as long as he made trouble. *Their loss,* he thought defiantly.

This particular purgatory was brought on by one of Finny's favourite pastimes – a spot-on impression of The Streak himself, the Principal of St Augustin's: Fr Donnacha Shanlon. Fr Shanlon was apparently an immortal – by all accounts, he had been in the school since before prehistory. You could find the yellowest, grungiest, antique relic of a photo in the most remote corner of the school and you could be sure the first person you'd notice in it would be The Streak, arching over everyone else like an imposing old oak.

He was called 'The Streak' on account of two things: first, his ominous height. Fr Shanlon, at nearly two-and-a-half metres, was definitely the tallest priest anyone in Kilnabracka, or, indeed, the whole of Limerick, had ever seen. At the crown of this commanding tree-trunk was his head – bald and large, it flowed towards the point of his hawk's-beak nose. Either side of this prominent bill, and squatting beneath hedgehog eyebrows, sat two dark eyes, sunk deep. His dark eyes occasionally appeared a vivid green, so that on the rare occasion you witnessed the light hitting them they looked like two gemstones set in some ancient gargoyle.

You only ever got to witness this when you were in real trouble – when he would take the bother to look down at you over the rim of his dense brown plastic glasses. This normally preceded an agonising pinch on the shoulder and an hour or two writing out sections of the phone book. Otherwise, he never really felt the need to come out from behind the cloudy lenses. His authority followed him like a shadow.

The other reason he had this nickname was on account of his considerable speed. This fleetness was not an obvious feature to go with such a lanky frame, but Fr Shanlon was insanely quick. His exploits in track and field were legendary, and there were countless stories about the races he had won and the games he had carried single-handedly: in his youth, whenever that was. He had also had some prowess on the hurling field. All of this combined to make him both respected as a coach on the pitch, and feared unconditionally, as there was very little you could get away with: The Streak would always catch you, eventually.

That day, not uncommonly, Oscar Finnegan had been caught red-handed. Finny, as everyone knew him, had a knack for impersonations, and 'Doing a Streak' was one of his better ones. He would crouch behind the teacher's desk, if said teacher was out or hadn't arrived yet, and unfurl himself like a giant plant opening to the sun, stepping seamlessly onto the teacher's chair as he did this, so that when he had stretched out fully he was (nearly) the same height as the dreaded priest. He would have borrowed his classmate Sam Flynn's ultra-thick glasses in advance, and the laughter would ascend from giggle to holler as Finny, transformed into Fr Shanlon, looked upon the class with exactly the right expression, the marker for the whiteboard held just-so. With perfect mimicry, he would open his mouth and The Streak's ominous voice would flow out of it. He had just time to utter 'Get ye out those books' in the priest's distinctive lisp, before he noticed that his words were met with total silence instead of bubbling laughter. He was just about to continue when he heard the real Fr Shanlon tell him: 'Get off that chair and come with me, Finnegan,' and the game was up.

Finny had always managed to find trouble wherever he went, at least since his parents separated when he was near the end of third class at St Edna's. Until then he was a regular kid – maybe a bit of a performer, and prone to make one too many jokes. The place he displayed most of his precociousness was on the pitch. Finny, even at that young age, was a serious talent with a hurley in his hand. He could weave around people like they weren't there, confusing and confounding the older kids he was encouraged to play with, and frustrating them unceasingly.

Towards the end of the school year, when fourth class beckoned after the promise of endless summer holidays, Finny's home life had taken a bad turn, as his parents decided they couldn't live together and be happy. He changed from that point on. What used to pass for cheek in the classroom swung into downright badness. He screamed back at teachers who hushed him. He tore up books and copies and paintings – not just his, but other pupils' too. Once he purposely blocked all the toilets with Mother's Day cards that his class had made, and didn't even make any attempt to distance himself from the act. He just flushed all the cisterns, and stood there in the overflowing water, hands by his side with a scowl on his face, waiting for the grown-ups to come.

On the pitch, he still dazzled occasionally with skill, but for the most part his game now was tainted with a nasty edge – a brutality even – and more often than not he was sent off for injuring an opponent not long after scoring a bewildering point or goal. His parents were called in, over and over. They came separately after the first few joint visits were rendered 'unproductive' by their bickering, and always with the threat of his expulsion waved in front of them. But the principal, Mr Brennan, was reluctant to give up on the boy, and knowing that his parents' split accounted for most of Finny's bad behaviour, decided to give him chance after chance. By the time Finny had started fifth class – having been held back to repeat fourth class – he had managed to tone down his outright destructiveness. But he had replaced it with a steady stream of minor disruptions, dotted with the occasional act of serious disobedience.

One thing he did have going for him were the friends he made that year. By being held back a year to repeat fourth class, he befriended two children from the Knockbally Estate (known locally as 'The Posh Place') and, against type perhaps, they became inseparable. For their part, the teachers and Finny's parents were delighted with his new gang: Sean Sheridan was beloved of the teachers, being so bright, and the Caddock girl – Benvy – was the perfect foil for Finny's wantonness, in that she would take absolutely no guff from any boy, being bigger than most of them. Sean's thirst for knowledge was infectious, and Finny's homework (if not his discipline) improved markedly after the little triumvirate was formed.

Then a funny little flame-haired American girl called Ayla had arrived to live with the big fellas. After a settling in period during fifth class, while the pupils of St Edna's sussed her out, Ayla had gravitated more and more to this motley crew of troubled sports-star, geeky bookworm and punchy tomboy. The gang of three became an indivisible gang of four.

And so their time at St Edna's came to an end, and secondary school loomed. Finny, despite the improvements in his attitude, was sent to the markedly more strict, all-boys St Augustin's School in the neighbouring town of Stradleek. The others, Ayla, Sean and Benvy, went to the 'normal' St Vincent's, at the top of the town.

St Augustin's prided itself on discipline and sporting excellence, but, despite their best efforts, Finny's behaviour settled into a disdain for the former and, what appeared to them, a complete lack of appetite for the latter. He missed training most days – usually on account of being in the familiar pickle of kneeling on a hardwood floor and getting a cramped hand from writing out sections of Fr Shanlon's ancient phone book.

Finny sighed and put down the pen, massaging the

pain from his hand. He looked around to see if Shanlon was about, stood shakily on aching legs and stretched. He went to the window, resting his chin on folded arms, and spat, for no real reason, on the glass. His eyes crossed as he watched his creation dawdle down the window, and then glanced towards the pitches where training was in full session. He reached into his pocket and got out his phone, checking the time and opening up the messages. No unread. He opened a conversation with Ayla and hit 'New Message'.

What u up to? S is my letter today ☹. What we doing later?

He scurried back to the floor when he heard the hall doors swing open, and looked like he had never left his task when The Streak appeared, telling him to: 'Go home and, please God, grow up.'

Taig and Fergus had almost got the last of the gear into the lock-up, and the toolboxes into the back of the jeep, while Lann made his final checks on the site. Lann looked in every room to make sure all the lads had taken their tools, and to switch off the lamps and check the generators weren't still running. He decided to leave the extension till last, frustrating as it was to look upon something that had been nearly a finished building, and was now practically just foundations again. He was in no mood to look upon anything that might aggravate him, as the odd feeling that had nipped away at him all day had by now grown to a ball of discomfort in his gut, with a fierce headache gnawing at the front of his skull. Lann still couldn't decide what it was, but by now it was impossible to ignore. Something was wrong with this day, and it was letting him know in no uncertain terms.

He hadn't realised he had walked out of the buildings and along the garden path until he found himself by the stone mound in the northeast corner. It lay hunched under the shadow of three tall and ancient birch trees that were covered in ivy, which also draped itself invasively over the rocks. He cast his eyes between the dark-green leaves, following the curving line of a scratch in the boulder's surface, and had just reached out to touch it when his phone sang out his infuriating ring-tone, with the volume far too loud (all Ayla's handiwork — so he wouldn't ignore it when she called), snapping him out of his semi-trance. He grunted and pulled the phone from his breast pocket, and saw the name on the screen: 'Oscar Finnegan'. He pressed the green answer button.

'Yes?' he said brusquely.

'Hello Lann, it's Finny here.'

'Yes, Osca— Finny. Sorry. What's up? I'm just locking up the site now. About to head home. Is Ayla's battery dead?'

'Yeah, I think so. I've been texting and ringing, no answer. Bit weird not to reply to texts, so I called to the house, but no one's home. I thought maybe she was with you? Just wondering if she's around this evening?'

Lann had turned from the hillock and had been making his way back to the car, but now he stopped, halfway up the path. The feeling in his stomach and the pain in his head seemed to be creeping towards each other.

'I'd say she's in her bed, Finny, and her phone's off or the battery's dead. You know what she's like when she wants a snooze. I'll tell her you were looking for her.'

'Yeah, but, she always answers a text – even if she's in a mood …'

Lann cut him off and ran to the car.

On the way home, as the mucky old jeep had broken every speed limit from Dundearg to Rathlevean, Lann had barely been able to tell his brothers what had come over him. Eventually, when they saw the whiteness of his face, and the clamminess of his skin, they looked at each other and guessed, without saying it aloud: Ayla.

The car screeched to a halt halfway through the driveway gate, and the three brothers nearly burst out of it and sprinted to the door. Even as they did so, each thought:

'We're going to look like eejits. She will be in her bed. She will wake with a start when the three of us stumble into her room, and fall back into the pillow muttering, "Ah lads …", because this had happened before.' And, glancing at his feet, Taig noticed the schoolbag on the floor and he knew they were going to laugh later. And Fergus saw her shoes on the landing and knew she was going to be cross with them for waking her, but they wouldn't care because she was safe. And Lann, when he thrust open her bedroom door, and saw the sight that had chipped at his skull and churned up his stomach, knew that she was gone. The thing he now realised he had feared the most since talking to Oscar Finnegan, or even since that morning when he woke with an unpleasant instinct about the day, was facing him: an empty bed.

CHAPTER 3

A Stifling Cell

Ayla jolted awake and gasped in thick, muddy air. She had that sensation of falling you sometimes get, except this one had lasted ages, like the fall was into something bottomless. It had not been a restful sleep, more like continuous fainting, and she had dreamt vividly about being back in the house, being smothered by her bedclothes.

It had now been an age since she had first discovered herself trapped in the clay cell. It felt like such a long time that Ayla felt utterly lost – mind, body and soul all adrift in the blackness. She had learned every curve of the walls, running her fingers along them, looking for the chink that must be there somewhere, feverishly scratching at the hard earth when she thought she felt it, and then pounding the walls with her fists and shrieking with rage when no gap was found. Each time she had given up the search and lost herself in sobbing. Then she just lay there, staring into the black. The ritual always ended with a bout of determination – a fresh calm to help Ayla look at the situation analytically and maybe find a way out. But at the end of this thread was always the creature, and all practical thought disintegrated with the memory of that twisted maw and hot coal-fire mouth. The vision of those eyes, like cold full moons on a bitter night, sent her scrabbling for chinks in the wall again, and the process was reset.

Once, Ayla had tried to eat the slop the creature had left after its visit. Her stomach still ached from retching. She had been so, so hungry, but it had taken her a long time to realise that the bowl of slimy rot was meant to feed her. At first she had pushed it with her feet as far from her as she could, assuming it was some form of torture, or intended to knock her out. But, as the hours gnawed at her, she became curious and reached out for it. Pulling it towards her, she had gagged.

Ayla was well used to pungent smells – a life in the country, living with three grown men, had seen to that – but this wasn't like the sweet silage that filled the air around Kilnabracka. It snagged where the back of her nose joined with the roof of her mouth and clung there, stinging. It drew tears and made her stomach heave almost instantly, but starvation made her curiosity strong, and she had sunk her fingers into the hot slime and brought a handful slowly to her mouth. It was thick, viscous and slippery. Semi-solid chunks slipped easily from her cupped hand and plopped back into the bowl. Ayla thought about her first time trying oysters, with Taig and Fergus shouting encouragement. How disgusting those little sea snots had seemed to her then. But if eating oysters had become like diving into the Atlantic in summer — this would be like diving into slurry!

She waited for a gap between surges in her convulsing stomach, and brought the entire bowl to her lips and drank. The slop slid down her throat as one mass, coating her insides with a slippery paste. It made her tongue spasm with its bitterness, and though she instantly spat out as much as she could, the putrid mulch clung to her teeth and mouth, leaving deposits of grit that would remain crunching between her jaws for hours. She had never in her life imagined anything so revolting. *I'll just have to starve.*

Without realising it, Ayla must have slept again. She woke with a cramping stomach and the lingering tartness of the slime in her mouth. It was even hotter and stuffier in her cell than before. As she shuffled for a more comfortable position it dawned on her that, despite everything, she would probably have to attempt the gruel again — it was that or die: black or white. In fact, she was going to have to be more cut-and-dry about everything from now on in order to survive. *Eat or starve, live or die, cry or think*

– no more messing or feeling all defeated. You may be Irish now, but you were a New Yorker first, and that's a tough combination. I'll try and try until the bitter end to find a way out and I will do it by making clear choices. Little girl, she thought, *grow up,* and she reached for the bowl. At her feet, light appeared.

Long black fingers gripped the edges of the widening gap and pulled the sides apart. Light flooded the cell and gripped the backs of Ayla's eyes like a vice, squeezing. She hauled herself to a corner and brought her arm up to shield herself from its piercing beam. Slowly, the ache in her skull faded and her eyes grew used to the brightness, but still she was afraid to lower her arm.

From the source of the light, cackling flitted through the gap and the light dipped once, twice and three times as her jailer was joined, to her shock, by two more just like it. One of them snatched up the empty bowl and hurled it across the cell, to explode in shards just above her head. Ayla leapt in fright, slamming painfully into the muck roof.

The three creatures spat laughter and moved further into the cell. They were small and deepest pitch-tar black – all apart from their two white disc eyes. Their bodies were crooked, with gnarled, sharp fingers and toes, unnaturally long. They had legs, arms and a head, but there was nothing else human about them, hunched as they were with cruelty and malice, and when one began to speak its burning mouth spat sparks. The other two again erupted in malevolent hooting. One carried a stick with a small, meek flame, which it waved at her goadingly.

Then the speaker turned to Ayla and let out a long, slow, hot hiss. Ayla couldn't yet summon the courage to speak, though she badly wanted to show some defiance. Finally it spoke: '*Little girl, far from home!*' The gaping furnace of its mouth sputtered, twisted into some sort of smile. The voice, guttural and rasping, bit at her ears. '*Little mongrel! Mewling little rat curled up in a hole so far from home she has no idea!*'

The other two cackled along and moved closer to Ayla, the one on the right, smallest of the three, bringing its face inches from hers. The heat from the vile creature singed her hair, but the smell was the most unbearable: when it spoke, fumes of pure rot filled the air in front of her: '*Yes, squealing runt! Whimpering ferret! Never see home again!*'

The third, who stood in the middle, joined in: '*Blubbering little slug, lost in a pit and half-dead in the dark.*' It laughed. '*But not to die yet!*'

The first creature spoke again: '*No, not to die yet, little rat! Not eating? Our feed not good enough for the little lady mongrel?*'

'*Pff! Lady Piss!*' seethed the middle one, and they all laughed.

'*No talk in you! Did you eat your own tongue then?*' continued the first.

'*Ungrateful weeping little stoat!*' shrieked the small goblin, with sparks from its mouth settling on Ayla's hair. She could smell the burning.

This was too much. From a swell in the pit of her stomach, Ayla found a surge of bravery and shouted back: 'I'd rather eat my own tongue than that wet dung slop! And I'd rather eat it twice than talk to you horrible evil monsters! Let me out of here or my uncles are going to rip you apart!'

She instantly regretted her outburst. She tried to backtrack, but her apology was stifled with a choke as the small goblin's knurled fingers gripped her neck. All three were close now, the fire in their mouths scorching Ayla's lashes and eyebrows, needling her eyes and evaporating her tears instantly. She held an arm up to shield herself and used the other to try and prize the sharp fingers from her throat. She could not break its grip. This close, the creatures' own eyes were a turbulent milky swirl, full of harsh light, cold and ghostly.

The first one, evidently the leader, spoke again: '*Your three fat oaf uncles are lost to you now, never to be seen again, little runt. They'll be dead from searching before they even come close. You're for the king and no one else. So eat, choking weepy piglet, or we will make you.*'

They left through the gap, taking the light with them, and leaving another large bowl of steaming slop. When

Ayla got her breath back, she winced in pain. The burns on her arm were already blistered and the pain in her neck still lingered.

None of the three uncles had spoken in the hours since they had raced to find Ayla missing from her room. Taig and Fergus sat in unblinking stillness at the kitchen table, neither looking at the other: just staring ahead into nothing. Lann was upstairs; he hadn't left the room and it was now heading towards evening. Fergus stirred and looked to Taig.

'We have to speak with Lann. We should have got going hours ago. She ...'

'She'll be nearly lost to us already, Fergus,' interrupted Taig.

Fergus looked incredulously at his brother, disbelief teetering dangerously close to anger.

'How could you say that, Taig? How can you talk like that?!' His voice rose as he spoke. 'Talking like we can't do anything. You know we have to find her!'

'I know, Fergus!' Taig shouted back. 'But how long has she been gone? Now that it's happened, where do we even start? It shouldn't have happened in the first place!' The last words scratched at his voice.

Fergus looked at his hands, clenched his giant fists and brought them down on the table. The fruit bowl leapt a foot into the air, the table cracked through the middle. He pushed back his chair and stood and looked up at the ceiling. 'We have to talk to Lann,' he said, making for the stairs.

Taig sighed, leaving the spilled apples to roll across the floor, and followed his brother to Ayla's room.

He found Fergus pleading with a stone-silent Lann, who sat on the floor leaning against the cold bed with eyes fixed at his feet. They were lost under his deep frown, and the only movement was the shiver in his jaw as teeth clenched and unclenched.

'Lann, this is doing nobody any good. We've wasted time now. It's time to move!' Fergus implored, frustration no longer creeping into his voice but coursing through it. He shouted the last part: 'WE WILL LOSE HER!'

Taig placed a hand on Fergus's shoulder. 'Lann, he's right. We know where she is. There is no sense in wallowing. We failed our first, most important job. We can't fail the second – we have to go and get her.' He spoke softly, ever the mediator.

Just as Fergus stiffened to shout again, Lann stirred and looked at them both. 'We have to talk to Cathbad the Druid,' he said, and stood.

The three buildings that made up St Augustin's were held together by concrete stitches, patches of mortar prone to crumbling and in need of repair. The dense cloak of dark ivy did more of a job holding it all together: in some places its vines even pushed through the walls, curling around ancient, clicking radiators and forcing wooden tiles out of place where it plunged down into the corner of a classroom.

Being so old, the structures had a sort of life about them. Dusty air wheezed through vaulted corridors; wooden panels on the walls ached and stretched and grumbled; hot water hissed through lost networks of piping, making them snap and shudder. Some corridors went so dark and deep that even the oldest priests claimed not to have been down them. Being out of sight to all, the stories of ghosts flourished, sightings became legendary and the bowels of St Augustin's were left unexplored by even the bravest pupils. To Fr Donnacha Shanlon, they were home.

Fr Shanlon had known the halls of his school – every tile and panel, buttress and pillar, sill and skirting – for so long that he had quite forgotten everywhere else. He knew he had been to a great many places at one time or another, but now even his dreams took place in the dusty carcass of St Augustin's. His rooms, in the lowest part of the Priests' House, were mostly quite spartan. An armchair and tall lamp were in a corner beside a table shouldering a stack of large, thick books; one wall was lined with more of these and on the opposite side two dark doors, to a small bathroom and bedroom, stood either side of a modest fire grate. Beside the chair, facing the entrance, was another door, permanently locked. This was the only room that held anything of great interest, but no one had ever seen its contents. Fr Shanlon himself had nearly forgotten what it looked like, if not what it held. The key never left its hiding place.

He had been sitting in the chair, quite awake and reading, when a dream had crept up and taken him. Where once he saw words on a page, now he was faced with a thick wall of mud. The room became hot and small, the air dense and sour. He could not move. From the solid dirt in front of him, tendrils appeared – finger-like tentacles of wood pushed through and sought his face. They were black, and they reached him quickly, cold to the touch. They wove around his face, creeping down his throat and up his nose, and then more came, but these ones were blood red and dripping, grasping for his eyes. They found them! Burrowing beneath the lids … but, in a millisecond, just as suddenly as it had arrived, the vision disintegrated.

He was in his chair, the book on the floor by his feet, the hand that had let it fall trembling. But Fr Shanlon did not gasp for breath or break a sweat. Aside from his quivering hand, he sat still and poised. He sucked on his teeth, glanced at his hand – the shaking stopped immediately – and let out a long breath.

A light passed through the room from the small window, scanning the walls and coming to rest on the locked door. The beams flicked off just before the noise of a puttering engine cut out and car doors opened and shut. The tall priest rose from his chair and arched his head back, then reached in to the roof of his mouth with his fingers. Three sharp tugs pulled the key from its hiding place.

The uncles had driven to the school in silence, but as they stepped out of the car into the icy evening, Taig was the first to speak.

'How are we meant to find him?' he asked.

'He'll know we're here,' Lann replied. 'Look, lads. It's been a long time since we spoke to him, so remember yourselves in there. Show respect. Show respect but ...'

'But never fear,' said Fergus. 'I remember.'

'Sure your wit and eloquence never fail to charm anyone, Fergus,' Taig added wryly. 'He'll be supping from your cupped hands before we leave.'

'Yes, and your rugged manliness might put the fear into him, Taig, as it does every housewife in Limerick. He'll be cowering before your blond locks and songbird voice within minutes!' Fergus retorted.

'A fine time for talk,' said a voice. It wasn't Lann's. He was looking just as surprised as the other two. It was close, like there was a fourth among them, but they could only see each other. Fergus blushed, immediately wondering how he could have joked when all this was happening.

'And a perfect way to alert the whole school. How do we explain three giant oafs driving around after school hours?' the voice continued.

'Who *is* that?' asked Fergus, spinning on his heels trying to catch the speaker. Lann stopped him with a hand on the shoulder and pointed to where Taig was looking. Across the gravel car park, a good forty or fifty metres away, they could make out the lofty outline of a very lanky man, hunched in a doorway and in shadow from the light behind him. His voice met their ears as if he whispered directly into them.

'This way please. Quietly.'

Fr Shanlon led them through a small corridor lit only by a reddening sun. It smelled of ancient varnish and industrial cleaner, musty and tangy. The walls were lined with photographs behind foggy glass, team photos from years gone by with rows of boys all in the same striped jerseys, hurleys on laps or held like rifles. Some smirked, others were deadpan and the rest grinned like maniacs. Every few feet there was a glass case housing teeth-baring ferrets, shark-eyed squirrels and velvet-feathered pheasants. One large case, containing a family of stuffed stoats, only survived Fergus's stumbling by Taig's light-speed reaction, who leapt and caught it moments before it would have exploded on the floor. Lann glared over his shoulder viciously, and spat 'Fergus!' between his teeth. The giant held his hands up bashfully and apologised. Fr Shanlon never turned or broke his stride.

They had passed through seemingly endless corridors, through door after door, until at last they arrived at a stairwell and descended to a level where there were no picture frames or stuffed animals. These halls were dark and unsettling; turn after turn, they tunnelled deeper into cobweb and dust. At last they stopped in front of a simple door. Fr Shanlon pushed it open and beckoned them through.

The three brothers stood awkwardly in the priest's humble room, glancing around and sizing it up. At least they could stand up straight, as the ceiling was high. No one spoke, as the lofty priest sized them up through his thick glasses, sucking his teeth and emitting a slow, quiet grumble. Fergus and Taig avoided his dark-green eyes, but Lann gazed back, chin raised defiantly.

'It has happened. She is gone, Cathbad,' he said.

'Yes, I know, Lann of the Long Look. You have lost her. You have failed,' Fr Shanlon replied, without a flicker.

Lann bristled, but said nothing at first. After another

long silence, he finally broke the tension: 'We have to go
and get her. We need your council.'

'Yes, I imagine you do. We'd better get on with it then.'

The priest crossed the room to the locked door, produced a key from his pocket and placed it into the keyhole.
The door moaned, resisting on rusted hinges. A breeze of
dank air brushed their faces, and made their hair stand up.
It smelled of dirty, wet stone.

The door opened not to another room, but to a cavern.
There were no walls but sheets of smooth rock. Limbs of
it rose from the floor or dropped from the ceiling, ending
in sharp points. The ground was uneven, and scored with
thin streams and rivulets. There was some light, cast down
through a small gap in the vaulted roof. It draped a blue
ethereal blanket on every surface, and made the brothers
look like ghosts.

In the middle, hulking around a clear pool where all
the streams met, were four tall stone plinths. They were
straight-edged obelisks, their edges marked with groups
of cuts and chinks, some angled, others straight. The pillars rose at least nine metres to the cavern ceiling, and the
marks ran up every corner to their peaks.

'These are Ogham Stones,' said Fr Shanlon. 'I shall read
from them, things will happen, and I warn you now, sons
of Cormac: you will be *afraid*.'

He approached the first pillar, ran a finger down the

nearest edge and began to read aloud. His voice slipped deeper as he read, and seemed to gather weight; pulling it to a tone so low it made the uncles' ribs rattle. The whole cavern hummed with it, sucking and swooping the chanting into the wet air. Pebbles danced and slipped from their perches; the water surface began to vibrate, droplets bouncing in time to a bass thrum that gathered rhythm as the incantation grew louder.

Fergus and Taig glanced at each other nervously, and they began to feel woozy. Lann tried to brace himself against it, but even he stumbled. Their heads felt compressed, like huge hands were squeezing them, tighter and tighter. It grew dark, just before the first phantom face, bearded and dead-eyed, appeared over a granite column.

CHAPTER 4

An Audience with Ancients

Benvy Caddock leapt from her perch on the wall, the whoop of her war-holler spooking a flurry of black crows into the sky. Her opponent was completely unaware of her presence; stupidly, naively thinking the area was clear of threat, he had passed along the wall, whistling, until the crushing moment he heard the shriek and turned to see her outline blocking the sun – impending doom in full flight.

With air flung from his lungs and stars dancing in his eyes, Sean tried to push his assailant off him, but had no strength. Leaning her elbow painfully onto his chest, Benvy smiled before plunging down on him again, squirting whatever breath was in him out into the cold air with a gasp and groan of pain.

'I'm bored, Sheridan,' the large girl, with rough, sandy hair tied back in thick waves, announced. 'I'm bored out

of my brain. What'll we do?'

Sean had been planning on taking his book to his favourite spot on the edge of the woods, but he couldn't say anything now: only wince and pray for some air to come back into his lungs. His glasses had fogged up and his cheeks had turned apple red. Benvy rolled off at last and sat up, hoisting his thick book onto her lap.

'*Elon and Xanadu: The Six Swords,*' she read the title aloud. It was written in elaborate, shiny type over an illustration of six swords in a circle, with lightning bursting out from the centre. 'Oh, my God, you are such a nerdlinger, Sean Sheridan.'

The boy hoisted himself to a sitting position. He took his glasses off and searched for a piece of shirt under his thick padded coat to clean the glass. Without them his eyes looked tiny and dark.

'I know,' he replied, still clutching at breaths, 'but we'll inherit the Earth. And you're a giant bully, by the way. You could have killed me! Book, please.'

Benvy considered flinging the book over the wall, but knew that would be taking the joke too far and just be a mean thing to do. She might enjoy terrorising Sean physically, but he was still her best friend, and had been all her life. She often waited for him here, on the outskirts of their estate, knowing that he would be slinking off for some quiet time with one of his ridiculous books. Sometimes, especially when she was bored, she hated the thought that he was quite happy to do something without her. She threw the book to him, and grinned.

'Let's text Finny and see what they're up to!' she said, flipping the leather flap back on her phone.

'No need,' Sean replied, pointing towards the estate entrance. Finny had just walked through, and was heading towards the Sheridans' house. Benvy got his number from favourites and dialled. They could see him stop and pull his phone out to answer.

'Hello? I'm just at Knockbally. You guys in?'

'We're at the back wall, bonehead, watching you shuffle through the gates like a hobo.'

He looked up in their direction and immediately started running.

'What's the panic?' Benvy asked, but Finny had hung up. When he reached them, he was breathless, suffering the effects of skipped training sessions.

'The state of ya, Finny! You—' Benvy began to jibe.

'Shut up for a second, will you?' Finny gasped between breaths.

Benvy and Sean glanced at each other. 'What's wrong?' Sean asked.

'It's Ayla. I think she might be missing.' Now he was looking straight into their eyes. He was not joking. 'I texted her earlier, but no answer. So I went to the house, and no one was in. At least, no one was answering the door. I know she might have been asleep, maybe her phone battery had died. But I knocked on the door hard. I was annoyed, thinking she was cross at me for something. I fecked a few stones at her window too: nothing. So I called Lann.'

Sean and Benvy said nothing, waiting to hear more, but they knew calling Lann was a brave move, and a last resort.

'At first he seemed to think that she was just having a kip and the phone was off. But before I could say anything more he hung up on me. Why would he do that? I'm a bit worried about her, lads.'

His two friends said nothing for a long minute, sorting the information, coming to terms with it.

'First things first,' said Sean. 'We go and check all the usual spots. We'll check in Coleman's Woods and head into town to Daly's. She could be anywhere. She's probably skipping through the woods, blissfully unaware anything's wrong.'

He tried to smile, but it was awkward. The other two nodded in agreement.

'Coleman's first,' said Benvy, hoisting herself over the wall, and marched towards the trees.

Deep under St Augustin's, three more phantoms had appeared, shimmering over the remaining Ogham stones: spectral heads of two men and two women, all corrugated and ridged with age. The uncles recognised them instantly: they were the 'Old Ones' – an ancient council of druids, feared without limit by ordinary people. It was they who long ago had set the task before Lann, Fergus and Taig. It was they who had given them the power to live without death. The Old Ones had been flesh when the brothers had seen them last, on the dark day the charge was made; Caer and Macha were the women, Aed and Midir the men. They were the true power in their time and even kings kneeled before them.

Now, they hovered above each point with blue light spilling in tendrils of heavy smoke from their eyes and mouth. Each was turned towards the centre of the stones, looking down to the pool where Fr Shanlon stood ankle-deep in water. His palms were outstretched, his face lifted to the ghostly figures; his own eyes and mouth infused with the same blue glow. The three brothers had stepped back into the shadows, stunned.

'*Cathbad, Earth-Brother, speak.*'

The voice, one of the women, Caer, was a winter wave sweeping through the uncles. It shocked every bone. They couldn't speak or move, held still and tight by the air around them.

Fr Shanlon answered, his voice still ocean-deep, 'Sisters: Caer, Macha. Brothers: Aed, Midir. The child has been taken.'

The cavern grew even colder, the ghost-heads, brightening but unmoving, fixed on the priest. One of the men spoke: '*Grave, unwanted news. If she is lost, all is lost. Her protectors? Killed?*'

'They live, Midir. They are here.' This was not a summoning – no one turned to look at the brothers. They still could not move, but fear was slinking into them, slithering and writhing behind their gaping eyes. There were no battles here in this stone limbo, no enemies to swing at, and no victory to relish: only fear. Taig seemed in more discomfort even than the others. He began to make choking sounds.

'*Then they die,*' uttered the second woman, Macha.

Taig's gagging intensified, gasping as the air was wrung from him. Fergus and Lann could do nothing, held fast. Their brother's body shook, a bead of blood slipped from the corner of his eye. His life was being crushed out. Still neither the priest nor his council turned to the uncles.

'*But first: they find. They know what must happen. They know they must search in the old places. They know they must go to the roots of the Earth. You will show them the gates.*'

'I will, Aed. She will be found. They will atone.'

Taig's quivering stopped.

'*We will open the gates,*' Macha spoke again. '*But know that they will only open for a short time. The first, as the sun is highest; the second as the sun is on the wane; the third as the sun has sunk to slumber.*'

The faces disappeared and the cave slipped into darkness; the brothers dropped to the ground, senseless.

Finny, Sean and Benvy strode along a worn path through Coleman's Woods. Evening sunlight fell in taut strings, rippling from leaves that sighed in time to the autumn wind. The undergrowth glistened with wet, and the gust showered them periodically with the water caught in higher branches. Occasionally the light disappeared as a herd of clouds covered the sun and soaked the trees with fresh rain. When this happened their view into the trees fell into gloom and the vivid green dulled almost to grey.

They had entered through a gap in the dense treeline on the Knockbally side and met one of the main tracks that cut through the centre of the woodland. The forest stretched from Dundearg to the eastern edge of town, passing both Ayla's estate and Benvy and Sean's. They spent a lot of time in there, and so each of them knew the network of trails in the sprawling forest well enough to alter their course without getting disorientated, and had covered most of the main walking routes with no sight of their friend. They were all tired now, but determined.

'Do you think it's time to head to town?' Sean asked. 'She's not here.'

'Hang on for a minute, lads, there's still a few spots off the main paths,' Finny replied. 'And she's hardly spent the whole day eating sweets in Daly's.'

'Maybe we should split up? Each of us take one of the back lanes; we have our phones, if one of us finds her,' suggested Benvy.

Sean shifted on his feet. He didn't like the thought of being alone in the woods when it was getting dark – his imagination could easily feed fears of creatures in the ferns – but he didn't want to lose face either.

'Good idea,' he said, defying himself. 'There's the track along the Famine Wall – I'll take that one.' This, he told himself, was one of his stupider suggestions: *take the path most likely to be haunted, Sean, like an eejit.*

Benvy looked at him sympathetically. She knew this sort of thing would make him nervous. But aloud she agreed, 'Fair enough. I'll go back to the big boulder and follow the badger track behind it – the one that leads to the small car park. Finny?'

'Ok, I know a place further down this way. We can meet in that car park when we've covered the trails, hopefully with Ayla in tow. I may kill her if I find her.

Text if either of you do first.'

He turned and set off along the main path. Benvy and Sean glanced at each other and parted, Benvy back the way they came and Sean directly into the mossy under-wood beside them.

Finny found the entrance he was looking for without even looking up. After walking along the main path to the top of a hill, and left through a tight corridor of laurels, he had arrived at a dark, bath-sized dip in the earth. On the far side of it a natural arch grew: pipes of wood thrust in a bunch up from the ground and arched back down to a crack in a green boulder.

This was a place that he and Ayla often came to together, and never told anyone about. It wasn't out of any malice that they kept it a secret – they didn't have many of those from the other two. It was just an unsaid agreement: this was for them, and no one else. They came for all sorts of reasons: sometimes to talk, other times to say nothing and sit in the green, cool light, listening to the whisper of moving leaves and each other's breath.

Finny always wanted to meet here when he was down or angry (which was often), fuming at some episode with The Streak or his parents. He would arrive swinging kicks at the saplings and shouting curses, spitting at the injustice of it all. Ayla would listen, offering bits of sympathy here and there, until eventually the fresh smell of the woods and the medicine of a good friend calmed him down. Then they would crack a joke, the tension would fade and they'd just sit and bask in pointless conversation. This little hideaway had been his best therapy by far.

Jumping the dip, Finny heard a shuffle and his stomach leapt with relief. He grinned, ducking under the arch and stepping into the hollow.

'I knew I'd find you here, you big eejit!' he laughed, 'You scared the feck out of all of us! I could kill you, seriously!'

He stood in the centre, still smiling, but his smirk faded when she didn't come out from her hiding place straight away.

'Ayla, stop messing, will you! We were all worried out of our minds, so this isn't funny.'

There was still no response. Now he was getting cross. She was being so selfish! Finny only managed to shout her name once more before a large hand covered his mouth and stifled his voice, and he was lifted off his feet.

The Famine Wall crept alongside the warped track, dipping and rising and wrestling with thick ivy. It was made of huge stones, wedged and stacked until it was a metre thick in places, the boulders shoed in clover. The light was poor now and it would be completely dark before long. Further down the track, Sean could no longer see the stones, just the outline in black. He was cold, and being no fan of the dark, especially deep in a forest at its most haunted point, he was really starting to feel peeved with Ayla and the whole situation. All he had wanted to do was read his book, go home, have a nice tea, and play Xbox until his eyes hurt. Now his friend was lost and he was alone on a grim trail with the shapes of witches and famine ghosts crouching in the shadows.

When a big stone suddenly slipped from the top of the wall, Sean's heart slammed hard against his chest and jolted him sideways. He tripped over a root and fell head first into a bushel of wet nettles just as a large silhouette emerged over the crest of the wall, and hovered over him.

It was a terrible phantom with a wild, shaggy mane that loomed just metres from him now and came slowly closer. Sean forgot the pain of the nettles, swallowed to keep his heart from crawling up his neck and began to whimper, shuffling backwards as quickly as he could. But the phantom moved quickly and reached out, pulling him up by the lapels. It shouted 'BOO!', and a grinning face emerged from the dimness.

When he could finally make sense of what had happened,

Sean knocked the grasping hands away and pushed Benvy back as hard as he could. She only retreated a couple of steps, still laughing.

'Benvy, for Jesus's *sake*! That's *not funny*!' he shouted, sniffing up loose snot and fixing his glasses. The nettle stings began to bite now, and there were lots of them on his hands and lower back.

'Oh man, that was *seriously* funny!' Benvy giggled. 'Your face when you went over! Priceless!'

'You're meant to be looking for Ayla, or have you forgotten? Would you rather give me a heart attack? That was so not cool.' Sean searched at his feet for a dock leaf and broke off a large one, crushing it against the white welts on his hand.

'Yeah, well, I knew you'd be freaked out on your own out here, so I thought I'd keep you company. Don't worry about thanking me! I should have left you to it.' Benvy was frowning now, secretly realising that maybe she had gone a bit too far, again.

Sean was rubbing a fresh dock leaf on his back when he noticed his tormentor's expression change. She had been scowling at him, but now her mouth dropped as she looked past him. She frowned and curled her lip, squinting into the gloom.

'Yeah, nice try, Benv'. You can't get me twice. You think I'm that stupid?' he said, but he turned to look just in case.

His eyes met a huge midriff, and travelled up its towering owner to a briar of red beard and untamed hair. Green eyes peered down at him.

'You need to come with me,' Fergus said, and turned back into the thicket, pushing trees aside like they were made of rubber.

CHAPTER 5

A Spiralling Path

The three friends were brought to a wide glade, walled by lanky firs but clear of any trees in the centre of the circle. The grass was tall and tangled, colourless in the moonlight. The last bit of day had faded an hour ago, and the clouds had melted away, clearing the sky for a bright, fat moon. A few stars shimmered in the night around it. It was cold, and the wind still pushed against the surrounding forest, making a noise like effervescence. Benvy, Finny and Sean stood with the uncles at the heart of the dell.

Benvy and Sean had been brought there in silence, with no talk from Fergus. They had walked for an age, directly through the trees, leaving the public area of the woodland far behind them. They had crossed over undulating lichen and moss, tripping over rocks and roots, squeezing through dense branches and scrambling up loose, mucky banks, practically blind in the gloom. It had felt like they were going in great circles, always turning left and never right. They had tripped through the deepening woods for two hours before slipping down one last wet bank, trudging through a copse of red-barked evergreens to their destination in the clearing.

When they arrived, Finny was already there, dwarfed on either side by Lann and Taig. He looked just as angry and cold as they were. When they were all together, Benvy and Sean glanced nervously at their friend, searching for an answer in his face. His eyes were defiant and cross.

'Well, we're all here then. Ok, enough of the silent treatment! This is freaking us all out and it's cold and I'm hungry and, to be honest, I'm pretty cheesed off, because this doesn't feel like looking for Ayla to me! So, whatever you're going to do to us, just do it! We don't know where she is, so torturing us isn't going to get you anywhere!'

Benvy and Sean were startled by Finny's challenge, but impressed. Their chins went up.

'Yeah. Eh. Enough of this sh ... shit!' Sean stuttered.

Benvy gawked in surprise, forgetting what she had been about to say.

The three giant men remained still for another tortuous minute. Lann was the first to break the silence. 'Fergus, fetch a stump. You know the type. Taig, clear the bracken from the stones, and show the lads where they are, so they can help.'

Fergus stomped off to the treeline and disappeared through the dark veil. Taig took off in the opposite direction, calling over his shoulder:

'Come on then. Let's do this quickly.'

When they got to the edge of the circle, there was a mound in the earth, thickly coated in weeds and brambles.

'What are we doing here, Taig?' Finny asked.

'You'll know shortly, Oscar. Better ready yourself for it. In the meantime, see along the edge of the clearing there,' he said, pointing along the line of trees to another mound just like the one they stood beside. Stepping up to the stack at his side, he grabbed a fistful of the bramble and pulled it off with one tug. Underneath was a huge stone, scarred with deep-cut spirals. 'You'll find another six of these around the perimeter. Clear the stuff off and then go back to Lann. Quickly, I'd say, is best, because it's getting dark.'

The friends threw each other a puzzled look, but still set off, each to a pile of briars, and gingerly cleared them off, snapping back their hands when a thorn sank in. Finny and Sean both revealed stones just like the first: branded all over with curved grooves. When Benvy yanked the weeds from her mound, she stumbled back in fright. A leering face, with a long tongue hung down to its chin, stared out, with two wide holes bored deep into the rock where its eyes should be. She steadied herself and looked around to make sure no one had seen her fright.

'Look at this ugly guy!' she announced, with a small shake in her voice, which she couldn't hide completely. No one took any notice.

When all seven stones were exposed, they returned to Lann in the centre of the clearing. He had been busy himself, clearing an area of grass and lighting a fire. It crackled and threw sparks into the night. He told the friends to sit and be silent before he began to speak.

'Ayla is gone, but not entirely lost. We know where she is. We need your help to get there.'

'Well, what are we doing here then?' Finny asked urgently, rising to his feet. 'Is she somewhere in the forest?'

Taig sighed and shook his head. Lann's glare, reflecting the fire in points of red, told the boy that speaking again would not be wise.

So Finny sat, and Lann continued, 'No she's not in this forest. She is not in any forest you know, or any place you know. There are things I am going to tell you that you won't believe. Then there are things I will show you that you won't believe. But they are real and true. And whether Ayla is found or lost forever depends on this meeting.'

'Ayla is not like you. She is not like the people in

Kilnabracka or in Limerick or in Ireland. Neither are myself, nor my brothers.'

Taig tossed a broken branch on the fire, throwing up a swarm of sparks, but the friends didn't take their eyes off Lann. He sucked in a long breath and continued, 'Taig, how old are you?'

His brother leaned back and looked up into the night, thinking hard. 'Emm. Let me think. I am four years younger than Fergus, and eight younger than you.' Lann nodded. 'And so that would make me ... three thousand, two hundred and seventy-three years old. Give or take.'

The friends looked blankly in his direction and then back at Lann, and then at each other. It wasn't funny. It was just getting more surreal by the minute. Why were the uncles joking around at a time like this? Why were they not panicking and searching under every stone for their niece?

Sean spoke this time. 'Ok, screw this! I want to go home now. I want to go home, and ask my dad to call the police and report a missing person and do this properly – the way it should have been done at the start. I want you to show us how to get back, and I want to go home because this is getting far too strange. Home, please! Now!'

He stood, glasses misted over in his fluster, and Benvy followed. They beckoned to Finny and turned to leave, just as a huge and sudden crack came from the forest in front of them, stopping them dead in their tracks. To the left, a treetop wavered like a drunk and fell to earth in a cacophony of snapping and creaking. Then a strange sound – the earth being ripped like paper – and the evergreens parted a minute later. Fergus marched towards them, carrying something huge on his shoulder. He arrived at the fire in ten long strides and dropped his burden down beside it, sending the flames flickering sideways in retreat. It was a massive, freshly hewn tree stump. It sat beside them, hunched on coiled roots still coated with muck. The wound, where the trunk was severed, was clean across, like it had been cut with a cheese wire.

'Spent ages looking for the right one, and sure, wouldn't you know, there was one only a few metres in. Typical.' He sat by Taig with a thud, clapping dust from his enormous hands. 'What are we talking about?'

'Just telling them how I'm getting on in years, brother.' Taig replied.

'Ah, I see. Mad, eh lads?' he said, apparently earnest, to the three stunned friends.

Lann was inspecting the stump. 'Well-found, Fergus. This will work. Oscar, Sean and Benvy. We three brothers are the sons of Cormac, warriors of the land of Fal – what you know now as Ireland. We are not Ayla's uncles – we are her bodyguards, charged with protecting her from a fate that has hunted her for millennia. Ayla is not who you think she is either. She is a person of great power, even if she doesn't know it herself. Ayla, you see, is the only key to a great and terrible evil being unleashed on the world. We waited more than three thousand years for her to arrive.'

Lann paused for a moment, and looked into the flames. 'The Old Ones – men and women of sorcery – saved us all by banishing her, unborn, before her power could be used by their enemies. She would live, as she had every right to, but in an age when her ties to that great evil were severed with time. We were given the task of waiting. Three thousand years we have lived. It took only thirteen more to fail. For that, our hearts are broken, but we must get her back, and to do that we need you. We cannot go back alone.'

Sean rolled his eyes and let out a short, disbelieving laugh.

Benvy stood again. 'You are all mental! I want to go now.'

'This isn't funny!' shouted Finny. 'We need to find her! I'm going.'

The three friends were on their feet and setting off away from the fire when Taig, impossibly quick, was in front of them, with arms out wide to bar the way and shaking his head. Finny bolted to the side, but ran headlong into the wall of Fergus, who looked down at him, eyes glimmering light-green, and ordered through his beard: 'Back, lad!'

They were set before the tree stump.

'See the rings, lads?' Lann said. 'As the tree grew, it surrounded its old self with the new. You can see the younger tree just by looking to the centre. Such is time. You can go back, you just have to "dig down to it", so to speak. We know the places to dig.'

Sean snorted. 'Time-travel? You're talking about time-travel? Let me tell you: time-travel can't exist. Believe me, I wish it did! I wish all of this were true, just like in my books. But it's bull!'

Benvy and Finny stood boldly on either side of him, shoulders thrust back in challenge.

'Total and utter ...' Benvy began, but she stopped short.

There was a noise, low and faint at first, but gathering weight. It was a hum: deep-seated, ocean-floor-low. It pinched the pits of the friends' stomachs and tugged at their ears. They looked to Lann and his brothers, and could tell instantly that they were the source of the noise. The giant men were barely visible now in the darkness, their right sides cast in orange from the blaze beside them, which glinted in their eyes like red stars. By now it was hard to tell one from the other; they were just impressions of the men, looming ever larger, black spectres revealed by the firelight.

One of them bent down to the stump and began to run a long finger along the outside ring, tracing it towards the middle. That's when the friends felt the hallucinations start.

'Hey!' shouted Finny. 'What's going on?'

'What have you given us, you *creeps*?' Benvy hollered, trying to retreat but finding she couldn't move.

Where the giant's finger went, the ring shone yellow and orange, as if it was being set alight in a perfect, thin curve. As the rings lit up, Sean noticed something in the corner of his eye: the stones on the perimeter copied the line, their own spirals glowing, like neon worms crawling across the rock in hot coils. He elbowed his friends to look, but the hum grew louder, pressing at their skulls.

The wind had picked up ferociously, whipping the tall grass around them into a frenzy. The temperature fell and threw icy rain into their faces. They huddled together, trying to lean against the gust, but it pushed them in all directions.

Benvy was the first to fall, only saved from being sucked away by Sean's grip on her wrist. Then all three slipped, holding tufts to anchor themselves against the tempest, which grew more violent with every second. The deluge swept against them, battering them in heavy drops so that they couldn't see.

And then, like a switch was flicked, it all stopped. The rain hung in the air, suspended in motion. Everything was frozen to the spot, paused. Even their clothes still looked like they were flapping madly, but without moving. And then the stone face, leering at the far side of the field, burst into light, beams leaping out from its eye cavities and shooting across to where the uncles stood, searingly bright.

The three giants basked in the white haze, and in the flicker of the dancing fire they seemed to change. They each had long beards now, and their hair was plaited and tucked into mirror-like, copper-coloured helmets. Leather straps were slung across their torsos, each bearing two swords in scabbards at their hips. Their waists were wrapped in heavy olive-green wool and thick leather, daubed in crudely painted spirals. All of their skin was tattooed with the same markings, whirl after whirl hewn into the flesh: scar and paint. They leaned on tall, heavy spears.

And then, in a moment, the light was doused and the hovering raindrops fell to ground in a single splash. Lann was hunched over the stump, and stood: himself again. No trace of crude tattoos remained; they were just as before. Fergus and Taig returned to refuel the bonfire as if nothing had happened. None of the friends could speak; they simply helped each other up and stared ahead, agape.

'That was the Truelight. You have seen us as we were,' Lann said. 'We know where Ayla is. She is a captive, and her prison is in our land, in our time. We can go back, but only so far. You must go back with us. You must be the ones to bring her back home. But before you do that, you will have to prove yourselves capable.'

Benvy was the first to shake herself from the stupor.

'You've given us some bloody drug! When my brother hears about this he's going to kill you!'

Her voice shook. Finny stirred himself and started to think frantically of a way to escape the giants. He stooped to the fire and grabbed a flaming branch, waving it threateningly at them. The uncles did not flinch. He threw it with all his strength at their heads.

Fergus caught the branch calmly, holding the burning end with no hint of discomfort. He tossed it back on the fire with a blackened hand.

'Run!' Finny screamed and hauled his friends by the wrists.

But Sean resisted. 'Why?' he asked the giants, holding his ground. 'Why do we have to go with you? Why can you only go so far?'

'Sheridan, for God's sake!' Benvy hollered, 'Let's get out of here! They're mad!'

'Why?' repeated Sean.

'Because we will not be strong enough,' answered Lann.

Taig pleaded: 'Ayla *needs* you to believe. If we go alone, she will be lost forever.'

The three friends looked to each other. Finny and Benvy couldn't believe Sean was even entertaining it for a second.

'We need to talk, alone,' said Sean.

'Of course,' replied Lann, and the brothers moved into the shadows, leaving the friends by the flickering light of the fire. When the uncles seemed out of earshot, Benvy spoke: 'You can't believe this rubbish!'

'We need to go home and call the cops,' Finny added.

'What just happened, happened,' Sean replied. 'There is no denying that. We saw what we saw. I doubt very much that drugs blow rain in your face and then make it stop in mid-air.'

The other two couldn't deny that the experience had felt as real as anything. But they couldn't bring themselves to believe.

'You only believe them because of those stupid books you read. Life isn't one of your dumb fantasy books!' Benvy said, a little hurtfully.

'Benv', easy,' Finny interjected.

'Yeah, well ... I believe there is more to life than we think, Benvy,' Sean retorted, 'And I think Ayla's uncles just proved that.'

Long into the cold night they argued, conferred, pleaded and debated. Then the uncles led them through the woods towards home.

CHAPTER 6

A Bright Light in
the Deep Earth

Ayla measured the time by counting endlessly. She had decided that trying to think of anything else was a waste of time. Dwelling on home only tortured her, and thinking on her predicament was even worse. The discomfort, the heat, the lack of air was all torturous, but worse now was the smell. She had to scratch holes in corners to go to the toilet and as she couldn't make them deep with only her bare hands, they had filled the cell with a pungent stink matched only by the goblins' food.

So she counted, putting *Mississippi* between every number for accuracy. She did it out loud, in a sort of chant that seemed to calm her. She also made up tunes and sang the numbers in rambling melodies. Worst was when she lost count. It shouldn't have mattered, but when it happened she screamed in frustration and sobbed, beginning all over again from zero.

The goblins had come every couple of hours, to throw in another bowl of wretched slop or a jug of gritty, stagnant water and to taunt her with ever more vicious barbs. When they ran out of inventive slurs, they jostled and pushed her, hissing in her face and scampering in and out of the opening to the tiny cell like excited rats. They seemed so full of hate for her, so eager to hurt and scare, restraining themselves only at the last second like rabid dogs on a leash and seething with resentment that they couldn't finish the job. Evidently, they had orders not to hurt her too badly. One goblin had screeched:

'*Oh to hurt you, little piglet. Oh to strike your face, bang your head, leave you for dead! But we can't. Such a shame! The king's orders! Only for now though, piglet. Your time will come soon!*'

Knowing that they couldn't really touch her didn't make these episodes any less frightening. They were so energetic in their contempt for her, bounding in and out of the cell like ricocheting bullets and hollering abuse. After each visit, it took an age to stop shaking. Then, when she was still again, she would commence the long and endless count to sixty.

After hours of this, the time-keeping became automatic. Despite her determination to concentrate on the numbers, her mind would wander involuntarily, and more often than not stumble into visions of the creatures. The two globes of their eyes hung aglow in the air wherever she looked, like sunspots, until there was no escaping them. They haunted her as she huddled in the corner of her cell with her head bowed between her legs, as if by curling up into a ball and not looking up she might somehow escape the nightmares.

The gruel was still utterly vile. There was no getting used to it, but occasionally and with a vast effort, Ayla had to eat it or starve. The food stung as it went down. *It smells like old diesel,* she thought, remembering the acrid whiff from her uncles' machinery. *Only stronger. This must be the most flammable stuff on Earth.*

After she'd managed to get it down, she braced herself against the convulsions, concentrating on keeping the slop in her stomach so as not to waste the effort by returning it all to the floor. It wasn't easy. Every bodily impulse rejected the porridge with gusto, hurling it back up her throat in protest. But Ayla's iron will kept the food down. When the latest bout of gagging eventually subsided, she lay back, totally spent, and resumed the counting of her inner clock. She thought about the smell of diesel again. And then she had an idea.

Finny, Benvy and Sean all agreed this was an impossible

situation. They couldn't deny what they had seen in the forest clearing, even though they wanted to. As they trudged back through the woods, led by the uncles, they had time to group and talk more about what was happening. It was completely insane: that was the first fact. And the second fact, which Benvy and Finny still only reluctantly agreed to, was that what they had witnessed was some kind of magic. The third, which they reluctantly accepted, was that if they wanted to save their friend, they would have to do what Lann asked of them.

Daylight had broken before they left the stone circle, and by now they were in deep, deep trouble with their respective families. To compound the problem, they were given very little time at all to devise their invented excuses (staying at each other's houses). They had to get home, grab some spare clothes, food and water, and meet back at Ayla's house as soon as possible.

Finny left with the uncles in their jeep. They would drop him home and wait for him outside, as he would meet the least resistance from his family. It was only his mother, and she generally tried to avoid any major conflict with her son, indulging, through guilt, his haphazard behaviour. She would probably be in bed anyway, he reasoned, and so he planned on just walking in, quietly taking what he needed and leaving without a fuss. It was Lann who convinced him to leave a note to say he had left for a match in Dublin and wouldn't be home for a day or two. The truth was, Lann said gravely, he mightn't be home at all.

Benvy and Sean had hovered at the wall by the forest edge for a while, plotting their own escape. They were in a panic because, in both cases, their parents may well have called the guards, and they certainly would have checked with each other as to the pair's whereabouts. It was almost eight-thirty am by Benvy's phone: their folks would have been up for hours, with ample time to work up a frenzy. There was no time left to deliberate now. They looked at each other, sucked in a deep breath and agreed to meet back at the forest car park in half an hour.

Sean slipped his key into the door and glanced skywards, offering a prayer, pleading with the gods that this might go without a hitch. Before he could turn it, the door swung open and his mother filled the doorframe, furious, while his father hovered behind her.

'Sean Sheridan, where in God's name have you been?' she shrieked, grabbing his lapels and hauling him into the hallway. She gripped him to her chest, kissing his brown curls feverishly, and stepping back to deliver a crack over the back of his head.

'Now, Sean, you had us worried sick. Your mother is beside herself,' his father added, while his mother delivered more angry kisses.

'Explain yourself this second!' she demanded, pulling him

into the kitchen. 'We were just about to call the guards. The Caddocks are worried sick too! Where is Benvy in all of this? What have you two been doing? Ah, God, Sean, you're frozen!' She was pinching his cheeks now and inspecting him all over.

'And the muck all over your shoes! And you're soaking! I could kill you!' she added.

'Your mother could kill you, Sean, so she could. Where were you, for God's sake?'

'Mum, I'm fine!' said Sean nervously. 'I told you we were staying at Finny's.'

'You never in a million years told us you were staying at the Finnegans', Sean.' His mother didn't believe him for one minute.

'You never told us, Sean,' echoed his father.

'I did! It was planned ages ago! I told you about it, eh, last week! I told you last week that Finny was having a … a party. For his birthday.' Sean gulped, 'And we were staying there for the night.' This was going to be a tough sell.

'Sean Sheridan, Oscar Finnegan's birthday is next month, so pull the other one. I know because Samantha is throwing a big bash at Quasar, and we're all invited. So, try again!' His mother's face was puce now, the relief fully replaced by pure anger.

His father put the kettle on. 'You'll need some tea to warm up,' he said.

'He can bloody well explain himself first!' his mother hollered.

'No, no, I'm grand thanks, Dad. I have no time, I have to head out again!' Sweat was forming in globules on Sean's forehead.

This was too much for his mother.

'Sean Sheridan, I tell you now, you are going nowhere until you tell me what you have been doing, where you have been doing it, and why your clothes are filthy and your shoes are covered in muck!' The threat in her eyes told of a terrible fate if her questions were not answered.

Sean needed to play this one like an Oscar-winner. 'Mum, I'm really sorry for worrying you. I honestly told you last week that we were staying at Finny's for our own birthday party – just me, him and Benvy. And Ayla, of course!' he added, over-enthusiastically. He made a mental note to kick himself over this later.

He struggled with an impulse to come clean and tell them everything – he never lied to his parents. But he continued, 'So we went there after school, and walked back through Coleman's this morning.'

'That explains the shoes, Mary,' his father said, and was shushed instantly.

Sean's mother looked intently at her son, boring into him, willing him to crack and tell the truth. The globules turned to rivulets, running down the creases on the boy's forehead.

'I also would have told you, I'm pretty sure, that today is the tour of King John's Castle. We're all going for history class. So I'm only home to change and get a lunch and then head to school for the bus. Then there's a film to watch about it or something, back at the school, like. And then we're going to Cashel.'

'Cashel in Tipperary, on a Saturday?' his mother asked, lip curled in doubt. 'Sean, I don't recall any of this.'

'We are, Mum!' he pleaded. 'We're going on a special history day, to Limerick and then on to Cashel to see The Rock of Cashel. And we're staying overnight.'

He could barely stop himself from wincing at his own lies. His mother's glare dug ever deeper, her frown burrowing down to the tip of her nose. The doubt was plastered all over her.

'I'm going to call Mrs Marnagh,' she announced, reaching for the phone.

Sean nearly lunged out in alarm, but was stopped in his tracks by the doorbell.

'That'll be Una Caddock. Jim, get the door, would you?' The phone beeped as Sean's mum scrolled through the contacts list, searching for the principal's number. She found it and pressed the call button.

Before the phone was at her ear, Jim Sheridan's voice

called from the door.

'Mary, you'd better come to the door. Sean too. The Guards are here.'

Sean's heart iced over and fell crashing into the pit of his stomach.

The creatures were due to arrive with more slop and vicious words any minute. Ayla's pinecone throat made it impossible to swallow. A hundred times she told herself: *This is a bad idea.* A hundred times she convinced herself not to go through with it. But each time, battling her own will, she determined that it was her only hope of escape.

She would have to be lightning-quick to pull it off, especially as her captors were so agile themselves. And even if she was fast enough, there was no guarantee it would work. Then she would surely be punished very severely for having attempted it in the first place. But it was worth it; it had to be. She waited in the dark.

When the first chink of light appeared in the wall, Ayla darted across the cell to crouch beside the opening, pressing herself back as much as she could to avoid being seen. The hole grew and cast more light in to the cell. Ayla held her breath as the first goblin entered, followed by a second – the torch-bearer. There was no time to think. As the first turned and saw her, she leapt, pushing herself off the wall as hard as she could, aiming directly for the goblin with the torch. In a second the first one was on her back, trying to push its long fingers into her eyes and nose, and gripping her neck with its other hand. But her arms were still free, and she lashed out at the creature beneath her, saw the flaming stick in its hand and grasped it.

A third creature was on her, claws digging brutally into her ribs as it fastened its sharp, hot teeth around the arm that held the torch. Her scream was throttled out of her by the creature at her neck, but she held on somehow and, even as a fingernail almost sank into her eye, she saw her target and pointed the flame to it. To her eternal surprise, the gruel not only took the small flame hungrily, as she had hoped beyond hope it would, but it erupted in a burst of white-hot light.

The screeches were deafening: wailing, squealing, hysterical shrieks as the black goblins flailed and thrashed around the cell, holding their eyes and cursing the pain. Ayla herself was blinded for more than a moment, and a deep cut stung beneath her left eye, but mercifully she had been saved from the worst of the flash by their grappling.

Desperately trying to keep clear of the thrashing creatures, she searched the walls for the gap. She elbowed one of them off when he thudded into her blindly, just as her fingers gripped the edge of the hole and she pulled herself out.

Her face pulsated with pain, but worse still was her arm: the deep bite was sealed with burnt flesh; blood and blister merged angrily, still bubbling with heat. Sight came back to her in flashes, just long enough for her to see a tunnel in the earth, strewn with the jerking bodies of blinded goblins. There were at least eight of them, two still holding their own dim torches and all writhing in sightless agony on the tunnel floor. Ayla staggered across them, kicking out when they reached to grasp her legs, and careened down the muddy corridor as fast as she could, stumbling headlong into the blackness.

'Are ye Mr and Mrs Sheridan?' asked the Guard in a thick Limerick accent. 'Parents of one Sean Sheridan?'

'Yes, Guard.' Sean's mother shouldered her husband out of the way, hanging up on Mrs Marnagh – just as the principal's assistant had answered. 'We have them home now, thank God. Apparently they were at a friend's house and never told us.'

Sean was pale with panic now. His bottom lip trembled. *What are we going to do?* he thought, frantically begging his brain for a solution. *Ayla needs us! This is taking too long!*

'S–Sorry for the whole mess, Guard,' he stuttered, 'but we have to be off now on a school trip. Thanks for calling, though! Protect and serve!' He winced inwardly at his last sentence.

'We know of no school trip, lad,' said the Guard. 'We'd have been notified of anything like that during our enquiries. I think I'd better come in to ask you a few questions.'

His mother looked triumphantly at her son, vindicated now in her doubt of the whole story.

'Come in, Guard. I'll put the kettle on. Jim, put the kettle on, will you, for God's sake?'

The Guard stepped in, removing his hat and wiping his feet on the mat just as the phone let out its shrill beep. Mrs Sheridan removed an earring before putting it to her ear.

'Hello?' she asked impatiently, throwing the Guard an apologetic glance.

They could all just barely hear the voice on the other end; it sounded cross.

After a series of *okays* and *I-See's*, Mrs Sheridan put the phone to her shoulder.

'I'm sorry, Guard, but it seems Sean and Benvy Caddock have a bus to catch.' She looked surprised, surpassed only by Sean's stunned expression.

'It's their teacher, Mr Fenlon, on the phone. Apparently, the bus will leave without them if they're not there in fifteen minutes.'

'I'll need to speak to him, please,' said the Guard.

Mrs Sheridan handed over the phone. The plump

Garda cast his eyes to heaven in exasperation, unable to get a word in. He barked, 'Well just tell us next time!' before hanging up the phone and throwing it to Sean's father.

Sean had no time to wonder. He just silently thanked the gods, and gave his mother a look of glorious smugness.

He raced upstairs to his room and filled a bag with extra jeans, a thick hoodie, fresh boxers and socks, and two t-shirts. He hesitated only for a moment before shoving his book into the front pocket of his rucksack. Downstairs, his mother had made egg sandwiches and his father had filled a flask of tea. She looked at her son with brow still furrowed.

'Be good!' was all she said.

'I will, Mum,' Sean replied, and threw his arms around her in a long hug.

When he met Benvy outside, she winked at him in celebration.

'We owe my brother two months of slave duty.'

'Two months, Sheridan!' her brother, Mick, shouted from his car, throwing the passenger door open for his sister. He was only a few years older than her, but he was spoiled rotten and had been given the car as an eighteenth birthday present. Benvy was never given anything. Mick was the great Caddock hope; she was just a girl.

'You can have three!' Sean replied, sliding along the back seat.

'What are you up to, sis?' asked Mick as they drove the short distance to Rathlevean.

'Nothing, Michael, okay? Just please say nothing to Mum and Dad, and we'll iron your disgusting underpants for as long as you like.'

'Sold,' he replied. 'Just look after yourself, alright?'

'We will,' she said. 'And thanks.'

The world was still waking up and it was beginning to rain when they arrived at Ayla's house. Inside, the uncles had packed small bags and were gathered around the kitchen table. Oscar sat amongst them, his own small backpack at his feet. Benvy and Sean felt a bit foolish with their giant camping rucksacks.

'You took your time,' Finny said, with no hint of joy. He looked nervous and pale.

'That would be the presence of the Garda Siochána, Finny,' Benvy informed him. 'But don't worry,' she said when she saw the concern on the uncles' faces. 'It's all fine. Long story.'

Lann stood up from his seat and walked to the head of the table.

'Okay, we're all here. We have no more time to waste. We are to go to the gates. We can only open them at certain times, so timing is all-important. Benvy, you will go with Taig to Meath. You must be there for sunset.'

'What?' she asked in surprise, 'All the way to Meath?

Where's the gate there?'

'Newgrange,' Taig told her.

'I suppose it's obvious really,' she reasoned.

Lann continued, 'Sean, you're to go with Fergus. To the Burren, to the Ailwee Caves. You must be there for the evening sun.'

'And you are sure of Ailwee, Taig?' Fergus asked. 'I could have sworn he said "Ardee".'

'Yes, I'm sure, Fergus. Cathbad was very clear,' Taig replied impatiently.

'It was Ailwee, Fergus,' Lann confirmed, 'For evening sun.' He turned to Finny. 'Oscar, you're coming with me.'

'Oh God, let me guess: the Giant's Causeway, the Rock of Cashel, the Blarney Stone?' Finny asked sarcastically.

'To Sheedys' farmhouse,' Lann answered, and slung his bag onto his wide shoulder.

CHAPTER 7

A Door in Time

I t was late morning when Lann and Finny arrived at the summit of Knockwhite Hill. The October sky was heavy and grey, and the air drenched the grass without a single raindrop falling. They had all left the house as soon as their destinations were set: Taig and Benvy took the jeep, having the longest journey to Meath. They dropped Fergus and Sean at Colbert Station in Limerick City on the way. From the station Fergus and Sean would get a bus to Ballyvaughan, on the north coast of Clare, and make their way on foot to the caves. Finny and Lann had made the short journey to Knockwhite, marching directly through the fields and the outskirts of Coleman's Woods. From the top of the hill, they could see out over the whole parish of Dundearg, and scan the Sheedy farmhouse for unwanted visitors.

The house was hunkered in a stand of trees at the foot

of a small hillock, about a kilometre or so ahead – too far for Finny to tell if there was anyone there or not. But Lann gazed out over the area in silence, arms folded and unmoving, before setting off down the hill without a word. Finny had realised early on that this would not be a talkative journey. He followed quietly, scampering to keep up with Lann's long strides.

They approached the farmhouse from the east, where the trees were most dense and the driveway was obscured by a thick ditch. Lann ordered Finny to crouch behind a tall, silver-barked birch, while he crept closer for a better view. Within a few steps, low branches obscured him and Finny was left alone in a drift of wet leaves. Minutes crept by, and Finny started to wonder if there was a point to this James Bond stuff. It was Saturday after all, so the site would be empty and this all seemed overly cautious.

Finny stood up from his hiding place, swept wet leaves from his soaked jeans and set off casually through the copse towards the main house. He could see a cement mixer beside a pile of grey blocks, stacked up against the gable end of the main building. Scaffolding coated much of the house. Beyond it, the courtyard lay carpeted with mud, flanked by half-finished stable buildings and beige prefab offices. There was no movement, and no sign of Lann. He called out: 'Lann!' before a wide hand covered his mouth and pulled him backwards.

Finny's face was wrenched around to face Lann, who was scowling with a finger to his lips. He pointed to the other side of the house, where a silver BMW jeep was parked. The boy's face flushed in embarrassment as he saw a man, covered head-to-toe in high-viz work wear and a gleaming safety hat, exit the prefab. He was holding a clipboard, making feverish notes while squinting around the site. After a minute, he ambled off, out of sight.

'We don't have much time,' Lann whispered. 'The gate will be open soon – at midday, when the sun is highest. We can't wait for him to leave. I'll have to deal with him.'

Lann signalled for Finny to stay put, emphasising the need to be silent with a warning look and another finger to the lips. He slipped noiselessly back into the foliage while Finny peered back out to the house.

After a few minutes the man in the high-viz gear appeared again, this time alarmingly close. He had walked around the main house, and now passed just metres in front of Finny's hiding place. The man was close enough to hear the scribbling of his biro on the clipboard and smell his sickly-sweet aftershave. Finny held his breath. His heart skipped more beats when he noticed the tall form of Lann prowling behind, looking for all the world like a lion on the point of pouncing. The poor man had no idea of the threat.

When the car door opened and shut, both men stopped

in their tracks. Lann's eyes widened, but there was no time to move. The man turned and his notes were pitched into the air as he leapt in fright.

'Jeepers, Lann! You scared the hell out of me!' he said when he realised who it was. The man's voice was an annoying drawl. He was obviously from the posh part of Dublin.

'Ah, Mr Fitzgerald. Sorry, I didn't mean to frighten you. I came down to check on the place. I see you're doing the same,' Lann said calmly, without breaking a sweat.

A young boy had opened the car door. He was about eight or nine years old, with white-blond hair. He carried a hurley and sliotar.

'Dad, I'm bored! Can I please just knock the ball around? I won't break anything!' His accent was just as grating as his father's. He didn't even acknowledge the colossal man who had appeared from nowhere.

'Lann, this is my son, Jarlath. Jarlath, say hello to Lann, the builder.'

The boy flicked a nod at Lann and bounced the ball on his hurley.

'It's as well you're here anyway, Lann: I want to talk to you about that bloody mound of rocks in the corner. It has to go! We want it levelled first thing on Monday, yes? We need you to put down foundations for …' he fumbled with the sheets of paper on his clipboard. 'For this:

a home office and gym.'

The architect handed over a plan of the new building. Finny could see the expression darken on Lann's face. His great brow scrunched in frustration and his sideburns bristled as his jaws clenched. It was obvious to the teenager that the big man was contemplating an aggressive solution to their dilemma. But it escalated quicker than he had expected. Lann crumpled the paper in his hands and reached for Mr Fitzgerald's collar.

Finny made his move, stepping out from his cover in the trees. 'Sorry about that, Uncle Lann,' he said, 'I couldn't hold it any longer. Oh, hi.' He turned towards the architect, doing up his fly and shaking his leg.

'Uh. Hello, young fellah,' Mr Fitzgerald replied, confusion scrawled on his face. Lann turned red, but before he could speak, Finny looked to the boy.

'Ah, a hurler I see! Mind if I have a puck?'

The boy looked to his father, reluctant to hand over his toys.

'Eh. Go on, Jarlath, give ...'

'Oscar.'

'Give Oscar a go. Lann, we can go and look at that mound.'

Lann cast a look of distilled rage at Finny as he passed; it warned of consequences after he had dealt with Mr Fitzgerald.

Jarlath, pouting, gingerly handed over the hurley and sliotar. Finny threw the leather ball in the air and caught it deftly on the end of the stick, turning it round in his hands and casting the sliotar behind his back to land again on the hurl in a blur of motion. He repeated a few similar tricks, expertly flicking the ball up and around his body. Jarlath's expression changed to one of beaming respect. Finny glanced to the scaffolding by the car.

'Watch this, Jarlath,' he said. In one flowing movement, he stepped forward, knocked the sliotar up into the air and swung at it, launching it high over the house and down on to a latch on a scaffolding pole. The catch flicked open, and with a groan of grinding steel it keeled over, pulling two platforms down with it, booming, clashing and clattering on to the roof of the silver BMW. Finny looked on in horror. He had only intended to knock a pole down. But the horror subsided with the need to move quickly.

Mr Fitzgerald's caterwauling holler rose above the bedlam as he sprinted towards the dust clouds kicked up by the fallen metal.

'My baby! My baby, are you okay?' he howled. 'Jarlath, what have you *done*?'

Jarlath hadn't moved, except for his shocked expression curling slowly in a gleeful grin. Finny looked to Lann, to tell him to run, but the big man was already at the mound, running a finger around the spirals on a cornerstone.

Sky and stone blended seamlessly in battleship grey, flecked with green. The landscape was a watercolour wash of limestone, distorted by runnels of rainwater on the bus window. Sean leaned his head against it, staring out into the lunar hills of the Burren. His trance was broken with a bump, as the bus careened up the narrow road and leapt on the uneven asphalt. He looked up at his companion, fast asleep and snoring thunderously, and shifted to try and get comfortable. But he was jammed in place by the snuffling red giant beside him, and returned his gaze to the stone fields rushing by outside.

Fergus had proved to be a fine travelling companion: a well of talk, anecdotes and stories, and an expert on many things around them. All the while in the car with Taig and Benvy, and standing outside Colbert Station in the drizzle, and for the first hour on the bus, he had barely taken a breath between tales of how those places had changed in the thousands of years he had known them.

For someone who looked so intimidating, he was a surprise; at the peak of this mountain of hair and muscle, there was a brain that bubbled over, but his enthusiasm couldn't mask the sadness in the giant's eyes. Sean was grateful to Fergus for trying to distract him from the seriousness of their mission; he could see that was the big man's ploy. But Sean's mind swam with thoughts of Ayla and what all of this craziness was really about. *What is she going through? What are we going through?* He thought of his friends. *I hope they're alright.*

He was looking forward to getting off the bus, though, that was for sure. He barely had room to breathe, wedged against the window. And while Fergus slept, Sean's mind had more time to fret, and that was not a path he wanted to tread. Best just to go along without engaging the brain, he told himself, and trust in Fergus. At least, unthinking, he could just take it as it came. Panic lay the other way.

Fergus woke as the bus rolled into the small town of Ballyvaughan and hissed to a stop. They stepped out into the crisp, wet air, and Sean allowed himself a long stretch while Fergus got their bags from the luggage hold. They set off through the streets without delay, making for the hills behind them.

'Right, lad. No more roads for a little while – quicker to go as the crow flies.'

'Why are we walking there, Fergus? There's buses every ten minutes,' Sean asked, although the thought of being crushed beside Fergus for another journey was not an attractive one.

'Because, lad, it's best you get used to walking. There'll be a lot of it from here on out.' Fergus stepped over a high gate as if it were a foot tall, and set off through scattering cattle. 'We have some time until the gate opens. Be good to have a talk.'

After half an hour, they had crossed through three farms, never erring from a straight path up the foothills, over stone walls and dense ditches. The grass gave way more and more to rock, and, after scaling one more wall of round boulders, they reached the base of a tall hill, the colour of oyster shells.

'Are you frightened?' Fergus asked earnestly, as they ascended.

'Of course I am,' Sean replied, short of breath. 'But I'm trying not to think about it. I think at this point I'm more confused than anything else. Bewildered, I think, is the word.'

'You should be frightened, lad,' Fergus said, 'and I don't blame you for being bewildered. There's a lot to get your head around, and there'll be more things to face. Stranger things. Dangerous things.'

Sean said nothing.

Fergus continued, 'We've told you what, and who we are. A headful of odd information, that's for sure. I suppose you could say it was totally unbelievable. But then, you have to trust what you saw. What Lann showed you.'

Sean thought back to the forest clearing, and the baffling visions they'd seen in what Lann had called the Truelight.

Distracted, he tripped over a deep fissure in the limestone beneath his feet.

Fergus was still speaking. 'We never trusted in magic. When we were young, I mean. Me and the brothers, we believed in real things, in what we could see in front of us. We were warriors and hunters, though not entirely ignorant of what some of those strange old druids could do. But we stayed well away from it, and concentrated on staying out of trouble. Well, at least *that* kind of trouble. The other kind – fighting and such – followed us wherever we went. Taig and his women, me and my mouth, Lann and his temper: these things meant a fight was never far away.

'But, in the end, there was no escape from those dark arts for us. We were sucked right in, chosen by the old men and women of magic – those druids, the Old Ones – to bear a heavy burden for the good of the child. For the good of everything, really. We had no choice, to be honest with you. And watching everything you know wilt and rot in front of you, all for the sake of some child that hasn't even been born yet? Well, it was a heavy, heavy burden. Too heavy at times.'

'But none of that makes any sense!' Sean pleaded. 'I don't know what you're talking about! Who is Ayla? Really?'

Fergus stopped on a lumpy slab of limestone, staring out over Sean's shoulder. The boy turned to follow his gaze, and gasped at the view. A sea of silver stone billowed out before them, heaving up into commanding bluffs and sweeping down in long curves to the writhing Atlantic. Rain fell as mist over Ballyvaughan, hiding the far side of Galway Bay in fog. The Twelve Bens peeked over the gloom, like hooded giants.

'The business of kings and queens and old druids and what they all got up to was none of our concern, you understand? But this situation involved *everybody*. There was a queen in the south: Maeve was her name. A sinister woman who dabbled with dark powers; we stayed well clear of her. Anyway, she had a husband, but took another man as a lover. Such things happened now and again, usually resulting in a battle or two, and the winner took all. But this union was cursed, and no one could have guessed how perilous it would become for everyone.

'He was an evil man, you see, this lover. And he too held a fascination with nefarious things. Their thirst for power became boundless; they goaded each other to darker and darker acts, immersing themselves in baneful magic. Together they cast the south under a hellish shadow, which quickly crept over the rest of our land like a pool of black blood. The Old Ones intervened and there was war, fought not with swords but with incantations. The rest of us were helpless, left to scratch a life out of a land under a foul veil, always with the fear that Maeve would win.

'At last, after a great effort, the lovers were defeated. But they couldn't be killed; their power was too great. Instead they were transformed, their *humanness* ripped from them, and were banished to the bowels of the earth to rot with the worms.

'But there was something the Old Ones hadn't accounted for, and that was a child. When they discovered her existence, just a babe in the womb then, they knew that that unborn girl alone held the power to free Maeve and her lover. Some wanted her killed, but good people, led by a druid called Cathbad, fought for her life to be spared. And so she was banished in time, to be born when the threat of Maeve was over. We were charged to wait. She was born thirteen years ago and she is Ayla: your friend.'

'But ...' Sean's mind spun with questions.

Fergus continued, ignoring him:

'We had waited and searched for so long, long enough for history to be rewritten a dozen times. And then we found her at last, brought her home and raised her as our own. But if we failed in our task ... Well, that's where you and your friends come in, lad. There are things you'll have to face that will haunt you forever, whether you succeed or not.'

'Hang on. Okay,' Sean struggled to compose himself. 'Leaving aside the four thousand questions I have for the minute. I mean: Ayla, unborn, banished in *time*? If we fail? What then?'

'Nothing then. Then you die. Then everything dies.'

They didn't speak again until they arrived in the car park of Ailwee Caves.

The gift shop was thronged with tourists, ambling between souvenir stands, browsing the coffee-table books and novelty pens. Fergus bought two tickets for the guided tour, and handed a red plastic disc to Sean. Their tour started in thirty minutes, so they had time to have some food and gather strength. Sean was starving, and wolfed down thick soup and brown bread. The journey had made him weak and slightly sick, and he was very glad of the chance to sit and recuperate.

When he had finished, he left to join the shuffling tourists in the shop, and bought a book with the last of his money. He forced the thick hardback *Symbols in Stone: Celtic Carvings of Ancient Ireland* into his packed rucksack, and met Fergus by the mouth of the caves, at the head of the queue. The guide announced the start of the tour, warning them of some tight sections to come, and the group muddled through the entrance and past the pits where bears once slept through the winter.

The tour took them through three caverns, each with their own spectacular features: the Praying Hands, the Carrots and the Frozen Waterfall all still held wonder for Sean, even though he had been there more than once before. In his determination not to think and just to follow Fergus, he never contemplated what exactly they were going to do once in the caves. As far as he remembered, the tour simply brought them back out into the open air at the far side of the shop. Where were they supposed to go? The guide began to speak, interrupting his thoughts.

'Now ladies and gentlemen, we'll soon be approaching the waterfall in the Cascade Chamber, so please be aware that you might get a little bit wet! Also, do duck your head as the ceiling gets a little low in parts. Some of you may need to bend over quite a bit,' he said, glancing at Fergus.

'We're going to switch the lights off in a minute or two, to show you what it was like when farmer Jacko McGann first discovered it, while looking for his little scamp of a dog.'

They stood on an iron bridge perched over a deep drop, into which thundered a gushing torrent of water. A spotlight beamed up from the bottom, illuminating the waterfall in an orange glow, making bright sparks of the edges. The guide had to shout over the noise.

'Okay, we're going to switch the lights off now, so anyone with small children, please hold them close. We won't keep them off for long. We just want to show you how absolute the darkness is down here.'

The lights clicked off, and they were in complete blackness. Sean waved his fingers in front of his face, but he couldn't see them. There was no adjusting to it. He was beginning to enjoy the feeling, when the most horrible thing happened. He felt himself lifted off the ground, and then falling, all so quickly that he never had a chance to cry out. When the spotlight came back on, it was beside his feet. The waterfall was drenching both him and Fergus, who still held on to the scruff of his neck. They were at the bottom of the hole, backs pressed to the cavern wall, four metres beneath the metal gangway. He could hear the guide above pause in his usual spiel to ask where the 'large gentleman' had gotten to, while Fergus held a finger to his lips.

'We need to go,' he urged, and stepped behind the cascade, beckoning Sean to follow him. The guide was now on a radio, urgently trying to explain that he had lost two of his party and calling for assistance.

'You can't miss him! He's *huge*!' the guide was saying. 'Well I don't know! He was just here. He's probably stuck in one of the tunnels!'

Behind the deluge of water, hewn into the rock, was a triple-spiral. Fergus began to hum, as deep as the caves, as he traced a finger along its curves.

Taig sang and told stories the whole way along the N7 motorway, then around the outskirts of Dublin and on to Meath. For three hours, Benvy was entranced and delighted by this entertainment, forgetting the long journey and even, at times, why they were on it. Guilt surfaced every time she laughed at a funny tale, or was so enamoured with his singing that any worry in her evaporated. By the time they reached the village of Slane, she forced herself into seriousness, and asked him what they would find in Newgrange.

'It's one of the gates, Ms Caddock,' he told her, mirthfully. 'The old ghosts opened them for us, so that we can go back. There's only a few around the place, and these are the only ones open, and only for a short time.'

'Old ghosts?' she asked.

'Ach, you don't need to bother about them. The Old Ones? They're that bunch of horrible old codgers that gave us this task in the first place. Not nice people, young Benvy. But powerful, that's for sure.'

Taig was always chirpy, always a word away from singing. But now, when she had time to think seriously about what was happening, Benvy felt it was a bit out of place. *Ayla must be so frightened,* she thought.

'You seem in a good mood,' she observed.

The smile dropped from the blond giant's face. 'Don't let it fool you, Benvy. I won't lie: I look forward to smelling the air in my own land. I look forward to taking a handful of wet grass and breathing in that sweet green scent, but I am hurting. And what we are about to do is so serious, you can't even imagine.'

'What exactly are we about to do?'

'We are going to go through a door in time, young lass. When we get to the other side, we'll be in Ireland; but not the Ireland you know. It'll be *our* Ireland – Fal: no walls or fields or brick houses or tarmac roads. Just land, green and wide. When we get there, we have to go to a place where I have hidden something of mine. It's my javelin, and you have to fetch it.'

At least a javelin was something she was familiar with, being one of her best sports in school, but she still couldn't quite allow herself to believe this connection to the past. However, she felt she had no choice but to go along with it, especially after what they had witnessed in the clearing.

'Why me? You know where it is; why can't you get it?'

'Ah, but sure where would the test in that be?' he answered cryptically. After a few minutes of silence he added: 'We've told you that we can't rescue Ayla alone. We need you, and Sean and Finny to help us. But in order to show that you're up to it, we had to leave our weapons under the protection of some pretty fierce ... *things*. If you can get my javelin, then you'll be ready to get your friend.'

'What kind of things?' she asked.

'I would say, young Benvy, that the less you know about that right now, the better,' he replied, and turned the car onto the main Drogheda road.

◎ ◎ ◎

A wide, squat mound, held up by a thick wall of white-washed stone, stood in the middle of a field. Under it was the famous Newgrange burial chamber. Taig and Benvy had parked at the visitors' centre across the river and taken the shuttle bus to the main attraction. The bus was full, and the mound was surrounded by visitors of all shapes and sizes. Some were even dressed up in long white gowns, and stood waving branches over their heads, swaying to beats pounded on a fur-skinned bodhrán drum. Taig explained that it wasn't simply dress-up; these people were modern druids, albeit completely misguided ones.

'Not an ounce of power! Sure they have it all wrong,' he said. 'For starters, they think there's some good in it.' But Benvy didn't quite understand what he meant.

While they waited patiently near the entrance, with a good ten minutes to go before their tour began, Benvy studied the strange 'druids' that were scattered around the field. They all had long hair and flowing robes, and nearly all of them carried those branches or banged on drums. They pranced around like shamans, singing to the sky and waving their bodies around with clenched eyes. *Bloody hippies,* she thought, casting her eyes up to heaven.

Then she noticed one of the hippies, a lady, had stopped

dancing and was staring directly at them. She looked different to the others – more bedraggled and dirty. She had wild, thick grey hair that shot out in all directions. Her robes were filthy and torn, and rather than carrying a branch, hers were stuffed into her gown, and leaves poked out from each sleeve. Around her neck she wore a stack of leather necklaces, all carrying oddly shaped stones and tangerine-coloured brass.

Strangest of all were the markings on her face: her cheeks and forehead were scored with wavy lines. Benvy couldn't take her eyes off her – this strange, wild lady that stood so eerily still amongst her gyrating cohorts. Her feral stare bore back at them as she started to move towards them.

A lanky young adolescent addressed the waiting group: 'Ladies and gents, we will shortly begin our tour inside the burial chamber. Before we begin, a quick outline of the history of Newgrange.'

'Taig, I think we might have made a new friend,' Benvy said, tugging on her companion's arm.

'What?' he asked, turning around. He squinted at the advancing woman. 'Oh sh–. Deirdre!'

'Taig McCORMAC!' the woman howled, pointing a long finger at the pair and quickening to a run.

'Benvy, inside: NOW!' he shouted, grabbing her arm and hauling her up the steps and into the chamber. The poor young guide was tossed aside, eliciting gasps in the flock of tourists around them. The sky dimmed and thunder boomed in clouds that suddenly gathered with unnatural haste. Benvy looked back to see the woman sprinting after them. Her eyes shone bright, vivid blue. She seemed to pull the thunder down with clenched fists. Taig dragged Benvy further down the narrowing corridor, their way lit in flashes as the sudden storm threw lightning after the thunderclaps.

'Taig McCormac! YOU CHEATING SWINE!' came the howl from the entrance, the wild woman filling it now, eyes aglow, and the air charged with electricity around her.

'Here!' shouted Taig, turning into a small annex that housed a broad stone bowl. The walls around it were engraved with zigzag grooves. He put his arms under the bowl and lifted it, turning it upside-down with a grunt of effort. It must have weighed thirty kilos. The underside of the bowl was marked with more oscillating lines. Taig put a finger to it and began to hum as the air around them filled with sparks. Benvy's sandy waves lifted above her head, and the fillings in her teeth throbbed as the wild woman rounded the corner and stood at the opening of the recess. The woman's expression held more rage than a hundred thunderstorms. Through rotten, mud-brown teeth she seethed, 'YOU CHEATING SWINE, RAT, WORM! I'LL K–'

And then there was darkness, before Benvy was dragged out of the void through a tight hole and into blazing daylight.

CHAPTER 8

A Map Misread

Ayla had run ceaselessly though countless bur-
rows, shafts, pits and passages, scratching and
groping with bloodied hands, blind in the inky dark.
Rough walls of stone and muck, laced with thick roots,
shouldered her aggressively as she scrambled, desperate
and breathless. Eventually, when her adrenaline faded, she
had to stop and be sick.

She had fled, haunted by the thought of her captors
right behind her, for what seemed at least an hour. The
tunnels had oscillated steeply, forcing her to clamber up
and slip painfully down on sharp roots and pebbles. Passages veered and arced with no pattern or reason; they
fattened to cold chambers and contracted to airless cracks
like the belly of a vast snake.

Now Ayla sat against the coarse wall, wiping sick from
her lips and tears from her cheeks. A chill draught cooled

the sweat on the back of her neck and told her that the passage was long. She shut her eyes tightly and tried to take stock.

I'm out of that damn cell. That's the main thing, she thought. *One thing at a time. Next: try to find a way out of here.* She had her breath back, but she still felt weak. *Just a few more minutes,* she promised herself. But just as she rested her head against the wall, she frowned. *Was that a noise?*

Then, there it was again. She lurched to her feet, straining to hear. There was no mistake. It came loud and long, ricocheting down the passage in a shuddering echo – the howl of those horrible wretches. She choked back fresh tears and ran.

Finny and Lann emerged, not into the daylight they had just left, but panting into crisp night, the sky deepest blue and pierced by stars. Finny rested his hands on his knees, sucking down air greedily, not even noticing his surroundings. He had a huge grin on his face.

'WOO HOO! Did you see that bad boy drop?' he laughed. 'Quite a diversion, eh?'

'If you ever get home, you'll be paying for that for the rest of your days,' Lann replied coldly. Finny's grin disappeared. 'But it was some shot,' Lann added, looking into the boy's eyes. Finny's smile returned.

'I never meant to wreck the poor guy's car,' he admitted, 'but it sure as hell worked! He …' His voice trailed off as he glanced up at the shimmering stars. 'Uh, Lann? Why is it night-time all of a sudden?' he asked.

They were on the side of a hill, which rolled down to undulating land like a black blanket. Finny could just make out an endless line of trees in silhouette. Behind them, a stand of huge rocks was fixed into the hillside. They were faced with complex spirals, cut deep. At the centre of the stones was a gap: the one they had emerged from. Lann drew in a long, savouring breath, and reached down to pull up a fistful of wet grass, bringing it to his face to inhale like the hair of a lost love. Finny watched the ritual, waiting for an answer. After a long moment, Lann muttered, 'We'll make a fire. Then I'll explain.'

He left Finny to clear a space in the grass, while he fetched kindling and a few large logs from the blackness beneath them. He was gone a while, and the boy shivered in the cool night, damp and bewildered. When Lann returned, he made short work of the fire, pulling flames from the woodpile within moments. Finny laid his coat down as a seat and held his hands out to the fire, shuddering as the worst of the cold left him.

'So? Where are we?' he asked.

'Home' came the short reply.

Finny threw his eyes to heaven, but before he could ask for a little more information, the hulking Lann cleared his throat, his face cast in the firelight.

'My home at least. My land – Fal. What is now known as Ireland. Actually, we're not far from what will become Limerick. But we're an age before it. We've gone back three thousand years, lad. And I suppose it's time I told you a little more about our story.'

Finny silently agreed.

The blaze danced in the uncle's eyes. He continued, 'Well, we already told you that my three brothers and I are old, thousands of years old. We are – or were – warriors. Good, for the most part. Certainly brave in battle. We had our bad moments too, but we always had our honour.

'Our father was a great champion. His name was Cormac, and he was respected and feared throughout all of Fal. He raised us in his image, taught us weapon skills and feats as soon as we could hold a rattle. Our mother died giving birth to Taig. I felt her loss more than my brothers, having known her longest.

'Our lives were spent on the land, always moving. We went from king to king, carrying our father's arms and minding his horses, until we were old enough to join him in the fray. We did that until the end, when he died beside me from a spear to the heart. Then we carried on doing the same thing, convinced we were honouring him in our violence.

It was years of this before I realised we weren't honouring him, but undoing all the good he had attempted. He had been trying to unite by the sword; we were just earning by it. We were paid most often in blood.

'When I decided we would lay down arms, my brothers were relieved. Fergus only really wanted to fight with his fists, for fun, and Taig cared more about music and women than any battle (although he was good at all of them). We spent a few years wandering, avoiding trouble. I found some land and we threw down some roots. Fergus and I both found wives, but neither of us were blessed with children. That turned out to be a gift. We thought our days would end like this. We were happy.'

He put a log onto the flames and they grasped it hungrily. Finny blinked against the sudden brightness.

'Of course we knew about magic things, and magic people. The elders of Fal were probably the only people we feared. They were called the "Old Ones" by us normal men. But we stayed clear of anything to do with magic or the magical realm: it only ever led to trouble.'

In the fire's dancing light, Lann told Finny the long tale of a conniving queen, Maeve, and her lover, and her power with evil magic. He explained how the Old Ones had imprisoned Maeve and her lover deep underground, forever.

The big man trailed off into silence. For a long time the only noise was the snap of wood being devoured by the fire. Eventually, he continued, 'Why the Old Ones chose us to sort it out, we still don't know. But they did, and there was no refusing them. There was an unborn girl, still in the womb, and she was to be protected at all costs. She alone had the power to free Maeve and her consort.'

'Ayla?' Finny asked.

'Yes, lad,' Lann answered. 'The old ones had used all of their power to send the girl away from trouble, to be reborn again, in another time. It was our task to wait for her and when she came, to keep her safe. It was a heavy burden. Our lives passed those of our loved ones. Everyone we knew died, and then everyone we came to know over the centuries died too.'

'Couldn't you just come back? I mean through the gates? To be with your wives again?'

'No, these gates are not always open. There are rules which must be obeyed. They had to be opened for us. The most powerful Old Ones – those who had fought and banished Maeve – they paid a heavy price for their victory. They had to leave their mortal bodies and become spirits. But even in their exile, they still hold great influence: it was they who Cathbad called on to open the gates and let us through.'

'Cathbad? Who's Cathbad?'

Finny noticed the corners of Lann's mouth twitch. It was the first time he had ever seen Ayla's grim uncle even come close to a smile.

'He's your principal, Fr Shanlon. He's no priest, lad. Even I'm only a fraction as old as that man. And he's not to be messed with – but I gather you know that much.'

The grin broadened, but only briefly.

Finny could only manage a '*What?*' before swallowing the wrong way in his shock, and fighting to regain his breath.

After a bout of hacking, he just managed to ask, hoarsely: 'The Streak? *The Streak?* He's one of these "old ones"?!'

He fell backwards into the wet grass and started to laugh.

'Oh. My. God. This is just mental.'

Lann placed the last log on the fire. 'I think that is enough for now. You should sleep. We have a long road ahead, and you will need all of your strength.'

Finny stopped laughing and sat up again.

'What can *we* do here? I mean, I want to find Ayla, more than anything, but ... Why do you need us? It seems like you could have done this yourselves, being warriors and all.'

'Sleep, lad!' was all Lann said, in that tone to which there was no answer but silence.

Finny couldn't sleep a wink, but lay still, staring at the

numberless stars, his head a storm of questions.

Benvy was only stopped from a fall of two hundred metres by Taig's hand grasping her arm. For a moment, his eyes looked down into hers and he held her there, frowning, before hauling her back up.

'Careful, young lady,' he said, as Benvy swallowed hard and let out a short shriek.

She had blacked out momentarily as they pushed through the gate, and when she came to, she was still in mind to run, afraid that the wild woman with lightning in her eyes was just behind. They had surfaced on a tiny outcrop on the side of a grassy mountain that fell vertically down to a rock-strewn valley, carved over eons by a noisy river. The drop would have killed Benvy.

'Oh, my God!' she exclaimed. 'I think I might be sick.'

Then, looking frantically behind her: 'Is she ...?'

'She's not coming through, don't worry. That was close though!' Taig laughed, and then stopped to inspect the land. He breathed deep, and a tear emerged from one clear-blue eye.

Long tufts of mist hovered low between the shoulders of mountains that stretched to grey lowlands at the horizon. Fat clouds dropped veils of rain here and there over the green. Dark forests clambered up the foothills, divided by the great glassy river.

'At last, I am home,' he said.

'It's beautiful,' Benvy said, still looking at Taig. 'But where are we?'

'Welcome to Fal, young Benvy. The young land that will grow up to be your Ireland. I have missed it greatly. It's been thousands of years after all.'

He lingered a while longer, savouring the damp air, holding his face up to the drizzle, and then picked up both his and Benvy's bags.

'Right, let's find a place to get warm and sleep for the night. Take care on the way down.'

From the small stand of rocks, a thread-like rut snaked down the mountainside. It looked treacherous. Thick tussocks of wiry grass slumped among the boulders, weighed down by heavy dew. There would be very little to hold on to on the way down.

'In fact, here.' He crouched with his back to her.

She stared blankly at him.

'Well? Hop on!' Taig offered again.

'What?' she exclaimed. 'Eh, no. I'm good, thanks.'

She took a step, and instantly slipped on a loose rock. Taig caught her for a second time, and resumed the crouch.

'Okay,' consented Benvy. 'But we *never* tell anyone of this.' And she hoisted herself onto his back. He smelled of wet stone and moss.

'Off we go,' he said, and began carefully picking his way along the narrow track.

After a while, the slope began to ease and Benvy was able to walk herself. They stepped through lead-coloured stones and knee-high grass for hours, until they arrived at a riverbank. Cold water surged over a small falls, roaring like a great crowd of people. Daylight was on the wane by the time they reached the outermost trees of a thick and silent evergreen wood. They found a spot with flat rocks and short grass, between a great pine and the bank.

'This'll do us, young Benvy,' announced Taig as he set the bags down. 'You go and get some kindling wood, will you? Small pieces, nice and dry.'

When Benvy returned, she found Taig had prepared a circle of rocks to fence the fire, and had fetched some bigger logs. When the fire was lit, he showed her how to make the seating more comfortable, using pine needles from the forest floor. Then they opened their packs and ate enthusiastically. When they finished, Taig filled their canteens from the river. It was the sweetest water Benvy had ever tasted.

'What do we do now then?' she asked.

'Well, first, we sleep. I don't know about you, but all the excitement back there has taken it out of me.'

'That's not what I mean. I mean tomorrow; I mean *next*. And who *was* that crazy woman, anyway? You said she was called Deirdre? And how did she do those things? With her eyes, and the storm? It was the most frightening thing I've ever seen!'

'Most things are frightening when it comes to magic, my young friend. That's why it's best avoided where possible. And as to who she was? Well, she was a ... friend. Once, a long time ago. I knew her, and then we couldn't be friends any more. It got complicated, and I am not a complicated man. She wanted to stay friends, so she wasn't too happy when I ended our time together. A lesson learned, young girl: never involve yourself with someone who knows magic.'

'So there are more of you? Back home, I mean. In our time?' she asked.

'Yes, there are a few around, beings who we would call "Old Ones". They are magic, and they were ancient even when we were young. I think they've been around forever, really. Not people you want to be mixing with – let me tell you. Although your friend Oscar has to deal with one of them on a daily basis, the poor fella. His principal, Fr Shanlon, is one of the oldest and most powerful around. Older than my brothers and I put together. His real name is Cathbad.'

Benvy could only gape in shock. But from what she

had heard of the lanky priest, it made a certain amount of sense.

Taig placed a log on the fire. It crackled in harmony with the river. The sounds of the place were all so musical: Taig's voice, the water and the wind in the pines. It soothed her greatly.

'As for tomorrow,' he continued, 'we have a fairly long walk ahead of us, I'm afraid. We're in what you would now call Wicklow, in the east. We have to travel south, and fetch my javelin.'

'So, what exactly am I meant to do with it when I get it? It's hardly the time for a throwing contest.'

'It's not for sport, Benvy; it's a weapon. One of my father's weapons, to be exact. But I carried it for many years. And then I had to hide it, in the hope that I would never have to retrieve it.'

'And why do *I* have to get it, then?' she asked.

'To prove yourself, young Benvy. Prove yourself or … well, pay the ultimate price, I'm sorry to say.'

He turned and lay down and closed his eyes. Soon he was asleep. Benvy never spoke, just stared at his back with a mixture of fear and disbelief fixed on her face.

Firecracker bursts of sheet lightning lit the land around

them in flashes of silver. Rain pelted down in the darkness between the bursts, while thunder peeled with threat,
like great steel drums slammed by giants. Sean cowered
behind Fergus, trying to avoid the worst of the cold wind,
but there was no hiding from it. They were already soaked
from the waterfall, and so the gale bit even harder. His
glasses were coated with rain, so he took them off, pointless as it was to wipe them.

'Something's not right,' the uncle said, his words stolen
by the gust as soon as they left his lips. 'Come on, lad. We
need to find some shelter.'

'Yes, please!' Sean shouted, but his voice had no weight
in the storm. He pulled his collar up around his neck and
followed Fergus down from the spiral boulders and into
the night. In the light of another bout of lightning, Fergus
could see a copse of hazel ahead. He held Sean's arm and
they leaned against the tempest, pushing their way to the
cover of the thicket.

They forced their way under the tangle of branches,
and at last found some respite in its centre. The gale was
broken by the hazel and it covered them from the worst
of the rain.

'There'll be no fire tonight I'm afraid, lad. Wrap up as
best you can and try to sleep it out.' Fergus pulled out a
heavy blanket from his pack. 'Here, throw this on you,' he
said, handing it to Sean. The boy took it gratefully.

'What did you mean back there, when you said something's not right?'

'I mean this doesn't feel right, lad. Where we've come out, I mean. I hope I'm wrong. We'll know more in the morning. For now, try to sleep, if you can.'

It didn't come easily, but after a time Sean slept, albeit fitfully.

When he woke, Sean was still sodden through. The ground beneath him had corralled rainwater into a thick brown puddle, and he had slept in it. He was freezing too. Fergus was gone, but his pack was still there.

Sean was grateful for the spare clothes he had brought, and though they were damp they felt infinitely more comfortable. When he had changed and packed away his wet things, he emerged from the thicket, putting his glasses on and stretching. His stomach growled angrily and so he wolfed down two of his mother's egg sandwiches. He decided to save the rest for Fergus.

The fields around him stretched away to the horizon, undulating slightly but otherwise fairly flat. Here and there, a grove of trees reached up to the now-blue sky, while several of them leaned over, broken by the storm. A few hundred yards away, the huge rocks of the gateway squatted on the grass, roofed by an immense slab. It was a dolmen, Sean knew, but bigger than any he had seen in books. He wondered why they hadn't just slept under that.

On inspection, his own books had suffered in the wet; the pages were wrinkled and limp. He decided to dry them out in the sun, and so set them on some hazel branches while he waited for Fergus to return.

It was an hour or more before he spotted the giant's hulking red frame coming back towards him. For someone so big, he was frighteningly quick; like a loping polar bear, those great strides covered metres in a single step. When he arrived, he went straight into the copse to fetch the bags.

'I don't like this at all. We need to move.'

'Why? What have you seen?' asked Sean, frightened.

'I saw a castle.'

'So? What's wrong with castles? Ireland's covered in them!'

'In Fal, lad, castles shouldn't have been invented yet.'

Sean struggled to keep up with Fergus, often having to break into a run to match his pace. They headed for the edge of a tall forest, a few kilometres away. Fergus wanted cover, to give him time to think. About halfway, at a small stand of oaks, Sean had to stop.

'Wait. Wait, please, Fergus. I need to stop,' he spluttered, between trying to take in deep gasps of breath. He collapsed against a tree and slid to the ground.

'Not a good place, young Sheridan. We need the forest, and I need time to work out what to do. I'll carry you.'

And the giant man reached down a great paw to lift the boy.

'No! No, just a minute, okay? I can go myself. I just need to stop for a minute or I'll pass out.'

Fergus reluctantly agreed to two minutes, and handed the boy a canteen of water. He paced the edge of the grove, watching out over the flatland, grunting to himself.

When Sean had regained some strength, he asked, 'Have we come out in the wrong time? And can we get back?'

'That seems to be exactly what's happened, yes. I *told* bloody Taig that it was Ardee! I could *kill* him! I pray that I get the chance. As for getting back, I dearly hope so. If I am right in where I think we are, I may know of an Old One who might help us. It's a big chance, but in this time, this particular fellow was never far from trouble. Right now all we can do is hope. And try to keep out of sight.'

'So, when are we?' Sean asked, in disbelief that this question should ever pass his lips.

'The castle has scaffold, which means it is still being built. But I'd know the style of it anywh–' Fergus stopped short. 'Why are you looking at me like that, lad?'

But Sean was not looking at him. And Fergus guessed, when the point of a spear blade pressed against his cheek, that the boy was looking past him to a man clad in iron armour. The hot snuffle of a horse confirmed it. When more men emerged from behind the trees with crossbows pointed at him, he knew they were in serious trouble.

CHAPTER 9

A Weave of Roots

Ayla had scuttled, crawled and clambered until every muscle was in spasm and her stomach swirled with fright. The passages seemed to branch off more and more; she could feel the openings along the cold walls, and she chose at random, in the hope of losing the creatures. Their screeches came from ahead and behind now, and desperation chilled her blood. She had no sense of getting anywhere, only of scrambling hastily to avoid capture. She had begun to slow, and then, despite begging herself for more strength, Ayla had to stop again. There was silence. She kneeled and closed her eyes.

When she opened them, Ayla was surprised to be able to make out her surroundings in the darkness. *My eyes are adjusting at last.* She could just see the walls of the passage, in places hewn from the rock into a rugged shaft, in others a mass of thick, writhing roots. She squinted and pulled herself to stand on quivering knees, curious to inspect the walls closer because – *yes* – where the roots gave way to stone the walls weren't just hacked at. They were lined with intricate patterns; long, thick lines interwove in an impossibly complex dance. As she ran a finger along one of the stones, she found to her horror that it ended in a fearsome face, with large, pointy ears and two wide, deep holes for eyes. Stepping back, she could see now that every surface was detailed with the same horrible mural – a twisted depiction of writhing goblins: portraits of her jailers.

Ayla knew that she would have to move again soon, but saw no point in blindly scurrying any more. There seemed to be a respite in the chase, and she needed to take advantage of that; she needed to take stock. Ahead, the passage rounded a corner. Just before the curve was an opening – a small one, more like a big crack in the wall. Behind her, it narrowed and dropped to the labyrinth she had just come from. There was no sense in going back there. She crept towards the corner, mindful of making any noise.

The details on the walls became clearer now, and the gloom began to lift. Her stomach twisted inside her when she realised why this was. Edging one eye just around the corner, she saw the passage widened, illuminated by torchlight. Gathered at its end were at least twenty of the creatures. She couldn't stop the gasp coming out of her, or the scratch of her foot on the ground as she jolted back from the corner. The wail came loud and long, piercing her bones. The others barked in unison, and one of them hissed: 'CAUGHT YOU, LITTLE RAT!'

Ayla made a dive for the little gap, cutting her sides on its edges as she forced herself through. She hauled herself down a tight shaft, choking on dust, which fell in sheets as she moved. The howls reverberated after her. After a few yards, the decline steepened and, unable to stop herself, she slipped down off an edge and fell headlong into the dark, plunging with a shock into an icy pool. The breath was ripped from Ayla's lungs with the sting of cold, and she stood in the knee-high water, gasping.

She looked around frantically. It seemed there was nowhere to go. The shaft above her flickered orange from torchlight. The high ceiling descended in a curve to the pool, stopping just a few feet above the surface. It looked like the pool continued down a low tunnel.

There was no other choice. She waded towards the overhang, the water climbing to her waist. By the time she was underneath the overhang, the water was up to her armpits and her jaw shuddered uncontrollably. The first set of glowing-white eyes appeared behind her at the shaft. She was about to take a deep breath and dive under when something coiled around her ankle, gripping it painfully. Before Ayla had a chance to wonder, she was wrenched violently under the water and into the darkness.

The knight's spear point never left Fergus's cheek as they walked. Neither did the nine crossbowmen ordered to surround him, marching in a circle with their bolts poised and pointed at his chest. Sean had just one such guard – a plump one, who didn't seem much older than him.

The knight, obviously in charge, had spoken in a language Sean didn't understand – a kind of guttural version of French. But he had seen their distinctive helmets before; they sloped up to a round peak with a single plank of metal covering the nose. Their captain, the one who held the spear so steadily at Fergus's face, was the only one on horseback. He wore the same chain mail as his men, but over it was draped a red tunic, fastened at the waist with a wide leather belt. It had three black lions stitched onto the front. At his side he wore a sword with a stubby handle, and from his horse's flank hung a long shield, shaped like an upside-down teardrop. He kept speaking to Fergus, but the big man said nothing. Eventually, the captain's patience ran out and he jabbed the spear, cutting a slice into Fergus's cheek from temple to jaw. Fergus stopped walking. He spoke to the captain in his own language.

'Sean, lad,' he said over his shoulder when he had finished, 'they think I'm a wizard and you're my apprentice.

For the moment I'm not letting him think any different. They're going to take us to the keep. Just keep quiet and follow my lead. Got it?'

'What did you say to him just there? And how do you know their language?'

'I told him he's going to pay for cutting me. And it's not my first time picking fights with Normans.'

Muddy faces peered out of fragile-looking huts of wattle and thatch, both curious and frightened. Beyond their straw roofs, the keep loomed on a hill like a sentinel, washed in red by the evening sky. It was indeed in the process of being built; rickety wooden scaffolding surrounded it, and builders still clambered as daylight faded. A tall fence of pointed wooden stakes, with a huge gate, stood around the perimeter, and more men with crossbows paced along the top.

The high gates opened with a groan, and they were ushered in. The grounds around the keep were thick with mud, dimpled by horse prints. Stalls were dotted around, housing chickens in cages and rabbits hung by the hind legs. Cattle lowed noisily. There was activity everywhere as people traded, talked, bartered and argued. The chime of a smith's hammer drew sparks from an anvil as he beat a red-hot horseshoe. There were pillories too, where one unhappy soul hung limp, his head and wrists held fast by a heavy block of timber. Everything stopped when they entered. Eyes bore through them as they were marched up stone steps and through the huge doors of the imposing grey fortress.

Inside was a grand hall, lit by flickering torches. The high walls were draped in tapestries, showing a hunt, a battle and, ominously, thought Sean, a hanging. Long tables ran up either side, with servants bustling in and out from doorways hidden in the gloom. At the far end, another long table faced them. Behind it, a high chair held a small, fat man with a bowl haircut and rings on each finger. He was flanked on either side by two other men in similar clothes, who leaned and whispered into his ears. There were soldiers everywhere. At the sight of Fergus an order was barked, and reinforcements flooded the hall.

The fat man addressed them in the same throaty French dialect, and the captain responded. Fergus said nothing. He had bled quite a bit from the wound on his cheek, and it had congealed in the brush of his red beard. Sean thought, for the first time ever, that he looked slightly weakened. When the lord and his captain had finished, the little man dismissed them with a flick of his bejewelled hand, and they were left surrounded by guards.

'What's happening, Fergus?' asked Sean, frightened.

'We're going into the pillory, lad,' the big man replied. 'And then we'll be hung.'

Before Sean could respond, he was jabbed violently in

the back by something sharp, and they were pushed out of the great hall and out to the bailey, where the last of the daylight was giving way to night. Torches were lit and handed to the guards, who forced them over to a wooden platform that held the pillories high up for all to see. Sean wondered why Fergus, so fearsome, was letting this happen. He couldn't stop the tears from coming.

'Fergus? What ...'

'Silence!' growled a guard in French, and hit Sean on the shoulder with the butt of his crossbow.

Fergus just looked at him and shook his head, placing his own neck and wrists on the rough grooves of the pillory. The heavy beam was lowered over him and chains run through the steel rings. Sean was kicked in the back of the legs and then hoisted roughly back to his feet. His head and arms were thrust into place aggressively. The wood gnawed at the skin, and already he bled where it chafed. Forcing his eyes up, Sean could see a crowd gathering.

The first cabbage hit the board just by his head, exploding in shards of green. The second didn't miss and his glasses were knocked to the floor of the platform. They were pelted, and not just with fruit. Some picked up bits of slop from the ground and hurled it at them. All the while the guards watched the crowd. Through squinting eyes, Sean was sure he could just make out one guard push a girl into action, pointing his crossbow at her until she reluctantly threw a turnip. After fifteen minutes of this, the crowd dispersed and night fell, fully. Sean found he couldn't help crying.

'Ah now! Fergus! 'Tis yourself!' said a voice from the other pillory.

Sean blinked in shock, and his tears stopped.

'Ah, Goll, how're things? Just the man I was hoping to run into,' Fergus said, feigning calm, but a quiver betrayed his relief. 'I thought I might find you here.'

'Eh, what is going on?' asked Sean.

'Sean Sheridan, meet Goll. Goll, meet Sean Sheridan.'

'Pleasure,' came the voice.

'Goll is going to help get us out of here, aren't you, Goll?'

'Ah, sure,' came the reply, 'why not, says you!'

Ayla slowly started to come around to the strangest sensation. Unsure if it was a dream or not, she didn't open her eyes. She thought she was in her bed and one of her uncles was sitting on her as a joke. But it wasn't funny; it hurt. And she found it hard to breath. From the waist down she was pinned, tightly.

'Get off me, Fergus,' she murmured drowsily, trying to summon the strength to wake up. 'It's not funny. You're hurting me. *Ow!*'

The last bit hurt a *lot*. She was fully awake now, and opened her eyes. It took her a second to make out what was happening, and when she did, she screamed long and loud in horror.

Around her waist were clamped two huge, fat, slimy lips. They advanced up her stomach hungrily. Above the lips, bulbous green eyes blistered out from a head that oozed with gunk. The fluid erupted from pores and warts all over its skin; they gurgled and gushed, occasionally popping with a sickening fizz. It was fat and wide and smelled horribly of tepid water. Translucent lids flicked up from the bottom of its eyes, first one then the other. It was an enormous toad.

Ayla howled and thrashed as much as she could. She bashed the thing on its nose and scratched and clawed at it, but it paid no heed to her, only swallowed faster. She tried desperately to reach its eyes, but they were too far back now. She kept hitting and punching, but the lips were nearly up to her shoulders and she couldn't breathe. She started to pass out again.

And then a light appeared behind the toad, there was a thud and the beast's grip diminished. Ayla opened her eyes, to see the shaft of a short spear sticking out from between those horrible eyes. The green light in them dimmed, and Ayla was so relieved, but only for a second, until she saw the small black goblins swarm over it. They removed the spear and hauled her roughly from its slack mouth.

'*Not for you, King Toad! This one's not for your supper!*' one screeched.

'*This one's for our own king, fat one! But you'll make a fine meal for us!*' howled another, and they all shrieked with laughter.

Two of them produced crooked blades and started carving slimy lumps off the belly of the carcass.

'Get off me, you horrible animals!' shouted Ayla, wrestling to free herself. But a creature gripped her jaws and put its face right up to hers.

'*We won't be letting you go again, runt! You're ours now, no escaping! Rotten, cowering, mewling toadfood! It's time for you to meet our lord king! He summons you to his court!*'

The last thing she saw was the rest of the pack bowing in mock sincerity before she was struck with the butt of a blade and cast back into unconsciousness.

Ayla was woken by violent shaking and the putrid reek of rotten porridge, a bowl of it being held under her nose. A gaggle of creatures surrounded her, in a large tunnel lit dimly by flickering torches. She looked around hazily. The ceiling was high and the walls seethed with the same horrid carvings she had seen before – long serpentine versions of the goblins, mingling in an intricate web. Here, their scrawny arms all pointed to one spot – an enormous, imposing door of steel. The door itself was alive with a carving of incredible detail. It depicted a thick swarm of goblins, like an army, all pointing upwards to a tangle of roots and on to a cruel-looking hawthorn tree surrounded by mountains.

'*Awake, little ferret? Good! A great honour for you now, my Lady Piglet! Stand up straight now! You have been granted an audience!*'

Ayla was forced to her feet. She struggled, but her elbows were gripped painfully. One of the goblins approached the door and placed a long finger into the eye of one of the sculptures. The huge doors swung open slowly and silently.

A cavernous, colossal hall vaulted up into cold darkness. Towering pillars covered in the same unearthly carvings leaped from the floor, impossibly wide and tall. To either side, countless more stretched off into the distance. Ahead of them, the broad gallery ran on and on like a highway, into shadow. There were torches here and there, but they did not illuminate the measureless hall. The light came from the thousands upon thousands of glowing white eyes that hovered among the pillar's feet like ghosts.

Ayla was knuckled in the back, urged forward. As she walked down the thoroughfare, the multitude of crea-tures on either side stayed eerily still. She expected abuse, howling, attacks, but none of them moved; they just stared. There was a noise, however; faint at first, and then louder as she trudged on: it was hissing. After a long march, she was stopped just where the light fell to gloom. The hissing had become deafeningly loud and then, like a switch, it stopped to dead silence. She glanced around and found their eyes all resting on her. Squinting forward into the bleakness, she strained to make out the scene before her.

High above her a furnace opened, hot and gaping, spitting sparks that danced like bright yellow swallows. Above it, two smaller fires appeared, dimmed and then opened wider. A booming, thunderous growl filled the air. All the creatures in the hall turned to the furnace in unison, and their light revealed its source. For a moment Ayla felt as if her heart had stopped; her lungs, her stomach – all seized by shock.

The furnace was a mouth. Above it were two flaming eyes. They were set in a face of blood-red roots, twisted into a grimace. The face belonged to a monstrous figure, an imitation of a man, thirty-odd metres tall, made entirely of the same gnarled, weaving branches that tangled themselves into the form of his face. He was sitting on a gargantuan throne of solid rock, his feet sprawled before him, his hands gripping its armrests like thick ivy. His head morphed into a crown, which spread like a fan from his temples and disappeared into the murky heights above.

The monster looked down to Ayla and the roots began to move, writhing into the shape of a brutal grin. It spoke: 'AYLA!'

The voice was like an earthquake. It rattled her bones. The air around her buzzed, her teeth chattered. A dull pain grew behind her eyes and throbbed.

'You are home.'

The hissing started again, reaching a crescendo as the doors she had come through opened again, and some kind of contraption – it was too distant to make out – was wheeled in. This time the creatures weren't still; they whooped and howled and scrambled over each other. The hall was filled with their caterwauling celebrations. The king leaned back on his throne. The contraption drew nearer. The king raised one tangled hand, and the crowd of goblins to his left parted, revealing yet another horror.

On the far wall, another being of roots hung limp and half-formed. It was a woman. Ayla could just make out a long neck extending down from half a face; the curve of a bosom; the slack form of a lifeless arm. It was grotesque. It didn't seem to be awake. Fresh tears began to flow down Ayla's cheeks. The scale of this nightmare seemed to know no limits.

The king spoke again: 'Prepare the loom!'

At that, Ayla was hauled backwards and then turned to face the machine that had been brought to them. It was tall, made from thick timbers and heavy stone. On a wheeled platform, two walls of granite flanked a raised wooden structure. At the centre of this platform there was a kind of bed in the shape of small person. Its arms and legs extended out in a star. There were belts of leather and chains to hold a person in. It looked more like an instrument of torture than a loom. It looked like something from which there was no escape.

The goblins began to chant in their grating, violent voices, louder and louder, to a shrill and deafening pitch. Ayla was shoved violently onto the steps and up, beaten over the head and arms as they wrenched her into the bed and fastened the straps violently tight. The chains bit at her arms and neck. Her screams were lost among the chanting. And then it stopped, and shifted to a lower tone, deep and baritone.

'Begin.'

The order came, and a goblin pulled a wooden device down over her torso. Instantly, the pain started. It felt as though she was being stabbed in the chest by a long needle, over and over and over. She choked on the agony, and just before the darkness took her she started to hallucinate. It looked as if one of the goblins had pulled a thread from her chest, tying it to a higher piece of the device. But the thread shone like neon, a glowing thread of white. It was the last thing she saw before passing out.

CHAPTER 10

A Test for Treasure

Lann and Finny had not spoken much as they walked. They crossed miles of forest, picking their way among the trees with barely a word. Finny kept some distance between himself and his guide. Any time Lann cared to look back and check, he saw that Finny was still there. He never lagged or complained – just marched in determined silence.

They had spent a full day on the move, breaking infrequently for a drink or a bite of food, and had rested one more night in the shelter of a great oak. Finny had barely slept again, his thoughts still overwhelmed by worry for Ayla and the insanity of Lann's story. They had risen early to a fresh, crisp morning, and quickly packed up and set off again among the dripping ferns. This time Finny had more questions, and this time he wanted answers to them.

'Where are the others, Lann?' he asked. 'Are they nearby?'

'No, lad, not near. Not even far. They're not here at all.'

'What? You mean it's only us? What are they doing?' Finny was frustrated at the thought of being the only one risking anything to save his friend.

'Calm yourself, lad. They're just as far from home as you are. But they have their own tests to complete. If you and they survive, we will go through another gate and meet.'

'If we survive? How can you say that and not tell me more?' Finny stopped walking. 'I've had enough of this strong and stern crap! You need to tell me what's happening and stop being so secretive about something I supposedly have to do and supposedly won't live through! What are these tests?'

Lann stopped but did not turn. Finny swallowed hard, suddenly nervous.

'Fair enough,' Lann said. 'I told you of my father's weapons. I didn't mention that they were magic. My father won them from a witch in Ulster, and they had powers beyond simple tools of war. This was either a blessing or a curse, depending on how you look at it.

'When we were given our order by the Old Ones, to live on and find the girl, first we were told to hide our weapons. We had to hide them in the most treacherous places we could imagine. For if it ever happened that the girl was taken by the dark forces that sought her, we would not be able to rescue her alone. We would need the help of three new heroes. These three would be faced with unimaginable danger, and it would take far more than bravery to succeed. Many heroes are brave and strong, but to rescue Ayla from the bowels of hell, they would need more.'

'Like what?' Finny pleaded.

'Love. Sacrifice. They would need the will to lay down their lives in place of someone they loved. And to have that conviction, that selflessness, they would need to find something else again. Their *true selves*.'

Now Lann turned to look into Finny's eyes.

'When faced with the ultimate evil, lad, only the true can triumph.'

He turned and began to walk again.

'The Old Ones opened gates for us, and taught us how to find the hiding places, and how to overcome the creatures that we would set to guard them.'

'Creatures? What creatures?' Finny asked, trotting after him.

'We couldn't just hide them under a rock, lad. Each is guarded by something abhorrent. The guardians are not men or women; they are the most fearsome things to have walked this world. There's a different beast guarding each treasure. They would never let the weapons fall into the wrong hands. I am sure, over the centuries, people have tried – my father's arms were famous. Those people would have died trying.'

'Then I'll die!' Finny shouted. 'I'm just a kid, Lann! You guys are the bloody ancient warrior heroes! I don't understand why you need *us* to do this!'

Lann turned to look at him again. He started to speak and then stopped himself. He swallowed, shifted the pack on his shoulder and said, 'Save your strength, lad. You'll need it. You'll be meeting your guardian today.'

With that, he simply turned and marched on through the bracken.

Taig stood before Benvy and looked at her with a mix of emotions. Among them, Benvy recognised pity and concern. He tried to disguise his feelings with a smile, but it didn't work. Behind her was the forest of white-barked birch they had spent the last day-and-a-half walking through. Ahead was a high inland cliff of granite, bright in the midday sun. At the foot of the cliff, a hundred yards or so ahead over flat flagstones and tufts of yellow grass, was the opening to a cave. That was where Benvy was going, alone.

'Why can't you come with me again?' she asked, a crack in her voice betraying her fear.

'This you must do on your own, Benvy. I can't help you. I can only wait, and pray that you come out again.'

He added, 'I have every faith that you will.'

This was small comfort. He hadn't even been able to tell her what to expect. Only that there would be a cave, and she would enter, and her survival was entirely up to her. If she did make it out, but without his javelin of red gold, then she had failed.

'Can't you give me any tips?' Benvy pleaded, already knowing the answer.

'I'm afraid not, young lass. You are on your own.'

He looked genuinely conflicted, and it seemed like a thousand thoughts were fighting for dominance behind his eyes. She could see him struggling with the urge to stop her, and she wished he would.

Benvy swallowed and took a long, deep breath. The air was fresh and quenching, full of the scents of woodlands. A gust carried a smell from the cave mouth: it was tepid and sickly. She didn't look at Taig again, in case it robbed her of what little resolve she had. *Am I ready to die for my friend?* she asked herself. *Why should I risk dying for something that's totally out of my control? Why should my life be gambled against Ayla's?* She thought of running, but realised she had nowhere to run to. She was in a strange land with no people or cars or telephones. She had seen *actual magic.* And she knew then that there was no going back. *Ayla is suffering somewhere,* she reminded herself. *Ayla needs my help. Ayla would do it for me.*

She inhaled deeply again, cleared her throat and began the walk across the stones. As she drew closer to the cave, the cliffs hid the sun and she was suddenly in shadow. The air chilled and sent goosebumps up her arms. The cold was coming from the black yawn of the cave mouth, and the breeze danced and swirled in the archway, creating a ghostly drone from the dark. When Benvy had just a few yards to go, she heard a shout behind her.

'Listen to the music!'

'Sean, lad, shut your eyes. Don't open them again until I say.'

The two men and Sean had remained uncomfortably jammed in the pillory until well into the night, to be sure that all but the wall-guards were asleep. Fergus and Goll had exchanged chat as if they were outside the local shop, but in a language Sean didn't fully understand. It was like Irish, so the odd word seemed familiar. Whatever it was, it must have contained some jokes, as they laughed together periodically. It was infuriating. Sean did as he was told.

Fergus watched the guards stroll along the platform behind the wooden perimeter fence. When they were out of sight, he made sure Goll was ready and that the boy's eyes were firmly shut, and his teeth and fists were clenched.

With a short grunt, Fergus lifted the top board with his wrists and the back of his neck, until the metal hinges groaned and snapped, scattering the bolts around him. Next, he placed a hand on each of the wooden boards that pinned down his companions. With just a modicum more effort, he lifted them both simultaneously and cast them aside like they were cardboard. Sean winced as he stretched the raw skin on his neck and wrists and, realising he could see barely anything, grasped for his glasses. One of the lenses was cracked.

It had been an impressive but noisy feat of strength. The night-watch guards raced around to the front to see what had happened and, after a moment of shock, howled for help. One started clanging a large bell, while the other fired a bolt at them. It whizzed just past Sean's ear, sinking into the broken timber behind him. The narrow windows of the keep blinked into light and its great front door opened. Soldiers poured out, drawing swords and loading their crossbows.

'Whenever you're ready, Goll!' Fergus shouted, pulling Sean behind him. 'Keep those eyes shut now, lad. And hop on to my back. Don't let go, whatever happens.'

Sean obeyed, clambering onto the giant's broad back and squeezing his eyes tightly. He had no intention of opening them until he was safe. As the Norman soldiers rushed with swords and a flurry of bolts rocketed towards them, Goll spread his arms and began to chant. Sean braved a peek from behind Fergus's red mane.

Goll was very tall – the same height as Fergus – but slight. There was no weight on him; he was gangly and long-limbed. His features were blackened with grime, his puffin-beak nose arching out over a wispy beard. He had his eyes closed at first, but then opened them, revealing a blinding blue light that stung Sean's own, leaving sunspots hopping behind his lids when he shut them again.

Goll's chanting grew louder and more frantic, and at his command, a fork of lightning hurtled from the night sky and struck the thatch of the smithy roof in an explosion of flame. The soldiers ducked, and some threw down their arms and ran, but more followed out of the castle door and down the steps. The captain was the last to emerge.

Fergus shouted, 'Eyes shut! Hold on! Don't let go!' before leaping from the platform and wading into the scattering soldiers. He swung his monstrous arms and hit two and three at a time, knocking helmets into the air and leaving limp bodies behind. He was ferociously deft, pounding his way across the yard, grabbing, lifting and slamming armoured men as if they were as weak as lambs. He carved a path straight to the captain, while thunder boomed and rain pelted down in thick arrows.

Round pellets of hail joined the deluge, as Goll's chanting grew in volume above the thunderclaps. The wound on Fergus's cheek had reopened, and leaked warm blood into his beard and onto Sean's hands. Still the giant strode through the soldiers, swatting them aside in groups until he reached his target.

The captain threw his sword aside and dropped to his knees. Sean didn't need to speak the language to understand that he was pleading for mercy. Fergus shouted something back, and then raised both his arms over his head. Just as he was about to bring them down, Sean shouted, 'Fergus, no!' and jumped from the uncle's back to stand in front of the begging knight. Fergus only just stopped himself, barely realising that his young charge was in his way. He blinked, confused, and then stared at the stricken captain. He hoisted Sean onto his shoulders like a weightless sack, and stomped away towards the gate.

Goll's incantation had reached its feverish peak, and his eyes blazed with waving fronds of electricity. Then he stopped, quite suddenly. The rain and hail and thunder followed him into silence and all was chillingly quiet. Fergus began to run for the gates, reaching them in a few long strides just as a deafening thrum cracked and rumbled overhead.

Goll clapped his hands once, sending rings of blue speeding from him in a wave of energy. Sean looked back towards the keep as Fergus ran, just in time to see the grey clouds gape in vivid light and spit ten bright bolts of white lightning down onto the keep, casting it all in fire.

For the last kilometre or two, Finny had noticed the forest change. Where they had been surrounded by curtains of green, leaves now curled brown and dying. The carpet of fern gave way to dense muck, and the hike became a monotonous struggle of pulling one leg free of the mire just for it to sink back at the next step. The trees, once tall and elegant, bent their backs like grey old men, while branches grew thorns that bit and jabbed with the slightest contact. Finny was able to match Lann's slow pace through the bog, and indeed it was the uncle who had to stop more than once.

Lann held out a hand and stopped again, this time slipping his pack from his shoulder. Sweat gathered on his angular brow, and he had to catch his breath before speaking.

'We're here' was all he said.

They stood on the lip of a wide basin, which sloped deeply down into a treeless bowl. The sky was overcast, but still sent light to the woods around them; in the dip it was dim and ashen.

'Down there, lad. That's where you have to go.'

Finny was very frightened. He didn't feel ready at all.

'There's nothing down there though,' he said, stalling for time.

Lann looked at him with his silvery-grey eyes. He placed one hand on the boy's shoulder. It was the first time he had ever shown any kind of warmth.

'There is, Finny. Go down and find it. I will wait for you, and pray that you come back.' He added: 'Be true to yourself, lad. That is the only advice I can give you. Be true and cast off the mask.' He said nothing more, backing away from the edge and leaving Finny alone in the dullness.

There was no movement anywhere. The air didn't stir, it was neither warm nor cool. Nothing rustled, no leaf shivered, no bird sang. Everything was still, frozen in time. Finny felt weak and sick. He wanted to run, or even just to lie down and shut his eyes. He wished he was home, and for the first time he stopped thinking about his friend. His only thought was that he should not be here; that the nightmare had gone on too long, too deep. Then, almost against his will, he stepped forward, over the lip and carefully down the bank.

When Finny reached the bottom, he could barely see in front of him. Whatever light hung above in the grey sky stayed there, silhouetting the ring of dead trees at the top. There was no sound, and the queasiness in his guts intensified, rolling in his stomach and weakening his knees. He took another step towards the centre. He heard the squelch of a step in the gloom ahead, and slowly someone emerged from the shadow, like a spectre through a wall. It was his mother.

'Mum!' he shouted, heart leaping with hope and confusion.

'Oscar, thank God!' she called back through tears of relief. 'I've been so worried! I thought you were dead! Thank God! Thank God! Thank God!' she laughed.

Finny wanted to run to her, but first, ignoring his own tears, he asked, '*How*? Why? How are you *here*? I don't understand!'

'I've been looking for you, love! We all have! I should have known you'd be here in Coleman's! But you've been gone for days. We have been so, so worried. Everyone is looking for you!'

Coleman's? He was in *Coleman's*? This was starting to make a strange kind of sense. He looked up to the edge for signs of Ayla's uncle, but there was nothing there except the shadows of trees. Had he been lost here all along? He took another step forward.

'You really were selfish in running away like that, love,' she said. The words shocked him, and he stopped. 'There's someone here who wants a word.'

And with that she slipped back into the gloom. A moment later his father appeared.

'Osc',' he said, with only a slight smile. 'We've found you at last.'

'Dad! You're here too!'

'We've all been out for days looking for you, Osc'. We haven't slept. Your mum's been beside herself with worry. You've really hurt her, bucko.'

'*I've* hurt her?' His face flushed hot with sudden anger. '*I've* hurt her? How about you!'

This was ridiculous, he thought. How can we be fighting about this now? He was just so happy that the nightmare was over, and that he could go home. But there was Dad, ruining it.

'I know I've hurt your mum, Osc'. I ran away too, I guess, just like you. But I came back. We were going to get back together. We *were*, until all this happened.'

Finny nearly got sick. 'Why are you telling me this?' he pleaded. He couldn't understand why his dad was being so spiteful when they should be running to each other. They should be hugging so tightly. It would be their first one in years.

Finny stuck his chin out. 'Whatever!' he spat, defiantly. 'I don't need you to be back with Mum. I don't need either of you!' He didn't even believe himself.

'Same old Osc'. It's all about you, isn't it, big fella?' said his dad, before turning his back and retreating into the gloom.

His mother returned. 'Oscar, why are you being so

nasty? You've already ruined our relationship; the least you can do is be grateful when we've gone to so much trouble to find you.' There was no love in her voice.

Finny choked back a glut of tears, but they broke through in a torrent, filling his eyes with salt. He screamed, 'I've ruined *your* relationship? *What* relationship? There never *was* a relationship! I don't need you! I don't want you! I hate both of you!'

The words left a bitter sting on his tongue. He wiped snot from his nose, scowling at his mother.

'You hate us?' she replied, calmly. 'You think we're *your* biggest fans? We were happy before you came along. We were free.'

Finny's heart felt like it was being stood on. He stared in shock at the woman in front of him. The woman that was meant to care for him, protect him, love him. He couldn't lie any longer.

'I do love you, Mum. I do need you. I need both of you. And I want you to be happy.'

'It's too late for that. Now come over here and let's go home. We can work out what to do with you then.'

His mother held out her left hand, beckoning him to her. He sniffed and walked towards her.

Wiping a sleeve across his nose, he could see her long brown hair, her friendly round face, those blue eyes that normally smiled but now were lined and grim. He looked at her outstretched hand. The wedding band glistened, despite the lack of light.

And then he knew.

'You're not my mother.'

The woman frowned.

'Oscar, don't be silly now ...'

'You're not my mother!' he roared and sprinted towards her. A surge of anger carried him forward, and he dived at the creature just as it morphed into the shape of his father. He landed jarringly and they both tumbled in the muck. Finny was agile and strong and sprang to his feet, pinning the thing down with his knees on its shoulders.

It was a sickening sight: a vile, featureless thing, twisting and changing before his eyes. It flitted between forms of his mother, his father; even Sean, Benvy, Ayla ... And then strangers: men and women and children. Hair grew in seconds and then receded; shoulders broadened and narrowed; the jaw shifted with nauseating clicks; skin morphed into tunics, armour, shirts, jeans. Its bones shuddered and snapped and rolled around the sack of its pale pink skin as it changed, all the while hissing at him and fighting to get him off.

Finny held it fast with all his strength until it stopped struggling and slowly reverted to its true shape. It looked at him with wide, ebony eyes. It had no nose, but a wide mouth full of pin-like teeth. It freed one arm and raised a hand, pointing with a long, thin finger. Finny looked, and saw a huge sword on the ground beside them. Its blade was wide, tapering near the handle. The grip was bound in leather, and the edge was lined with kinks.

He readied himself and, as quick as he could, pushed himself off the creature and scrambled over to the blade and lifted it. It was surprisingly light. He waved it threateningly at the monster.

'Come on then!' he shouted.

The creature looked back at him, blinked once and began to shudder noisily. Bones clacked and flesh sucked, stretching and sinking and folding, until Finny stood facing a clone of himself. The doppelganger sneered, and spat on the ground between them. It paced, growing angrier with every step, and spat again, its face puce with rage, the teeth still needle-sharp. It shouted at the air in guttural barks that made little sense but for one word: *hate*. Finny recognised the fury in the creature; could feel it gurgling inside him too, like a thick, boiling soup. It filled him with the urge to thrash and rip and stamp.

'*Stop!*' he shouted, and the thing did just the same, spitting the word back in perfect unison.

'*Stop!*' he screamed again, and still the creature matched him like a mirror. Finny burned with loathing of this twisted, vile version of himself. He wanted to hack at it, to beat it down and never face it again.

Then all at once the thing stopped. It retreated back to the shadows, with a menacing smile that jarred Finny out of his wrath. A second later, it emerged again, holding a sword, just like the one Finny had. Finny looked down. He was holding a branch that swarmed with woodlice. He dropped the branch in horror and watched it melt away, gorged on by the lice that then scurried away into the mud. The thing seemed to *laugh*. And then it lunged at Finny.

It swung the blade of its sword in wild, angry arcs, as Finny stumbled back and fell over his own feet. He rolled away just as the creature brought the sword down, and down again, in frantic, blood-hungry chops. Finny found time to scamper away when the thing struggled for a moment to release its weapon from the mud.

He saw the creature's flesh quiver and bones shunt again for one final horror: it took the form of Ayla. With the sword freed, it approached Finny again to resume its frenzy. The fact that it looked like his lost friend sickened Finny to the pit of his stomach. There was no more time for him to panic, nor anywhere for him to run. *If I die then Ayla dies,* he told himself, surprised by his own momentary calm. He ran at the thing headlong.

Diving under the blade as it cleaved the air over his head, Finny muscled in right under the monster's nose, refusing to look at the contorted likeness of Ayla, allowing instinct to drive his movements.

In close, he suddenly felt in a kind of control. He imagined himself in a match, fighting against bigger lads and bigger odds as always. He ducked and side-stepped and twirled among the thrashing limbs, driving his elbow into the creature's side when he could, and kicking out at its ankles. Then he would sprint out, avoid a swinging arm and circle the thing. He picked his moments to attack, diving in when he knew his opponent was flustered.

The creature grew more rabid with every blow, forgetting to hold onto any kind of form and instead twisting itself into a demented mess of half-formed people. Finny shouldered and pushed, always just evading the blows at the last second. He was waiting for the perfect moment.

In its tantrum the thing lost its grip on the sword. Finny saw his chance and hit at the butt of the hilt, then threw himself at the weapon on the ground. When he held it aloft, the blade seemed to light up, just for a second in a flush of blue, before the creature threw itself down to crush the boy and, in doing so, skewered itself straight through the chest. It gurgled out its last breath in a slow trickle of black blood.

Finny hauled himself from under the dead creature and lay in the mud, struggling for breath. Then he climbed back up the bank with his prize. At the top, a strong arm was waiting to haul him up. Lann smiled at him for only the second time, and took Finny into his arms in a long embrace.

Inside, the cave was icy cold. Benvy's breath came out in plumes, and her jaw began to chatter uncontrollably. She pulled her hood over her head and her sleeves over her hands, tucking them under her armpits. Her eyes adjusted slightly to the murky light, and she could make out the cavern walls, glistening with wet. The tunnel went downwards, and her fear grew with every step. Still she moved forward.

At the bottom of a slope, the passage levelled out and opened into a vast cavern. Drops of water echoed as they plopped into deep pools. At the far side was a smaller opening, and from this yellow light flickered. An urge to turn and run surged through Benvy, but she resisted. *I bet they expect the girl to run. I bet Taig wished he had taken Finny or even Sean. I bet they're just waiting for me to fail.* She walked on between the pools.

When she reached the opening, she fought one more powerful compulsion to leave as quickly as she could. She bit her lip and closed her eyes. *Come on Benvy. Show them.*

She went in.

She found herself in a large room, where the walls were hewn into pillars and alcoves. At the top, between two pots of fire, there was a boulder of marble, cut cleanly in half. Splashes of gold shimmered in the firelight on its rough flanks. Sitting on top was a woman – at least a sort of woman. She was naked and beautiful, but her forehead was unnaturally high and two long, curved horns sprung from it in a graceful arc. Her ears were like an animal's; a cow's or a goat's perhaps, falling at right angles from her head. They flicked and moved independently. Her eyes were thin and wide and yellow, with black slits for pupils. She rested one long-fingered hand on a huge harp beside her. It was made of bones.

'Greetings, Benvy Caddock,' she said. Her voice was sonorous and smooth. It fell on Benvy's ears like syrup. Benvy was still afraid, but felt inexplicably a little more at ease.

'Hello,' Benvy responded, 'I mean, uh, greetings.'

'You have come for the javelin of Taig McCormac, yes?'

'Em, yes. Yes, I have.'

This was easy, so far.

'Good. We will get to that soon. First, let us talk.'

Benvy thought talking to this woman wouldn't be too bad.

'You are a heavy-set young thing, aren't you?'

Benvy blushed, but she was not offended. It was the truth.

'Em, yes. I guess so.'

'But you would like to grow to be very beautiful?'

'I don't really care about that stuff,' Benvy said, bashfully.

'Don't you? You don't care that you are more like a boy?'

These words carried a little more sting than before.

'I'm not ...' Benvy frowned now. The woman was right, of course, but it did hurt a little.

'I'm sorry, child. I don't mean to offend you. I have seen you bloom, Benvy Caddock, as a young woman. And I have seen you age like a willow, bowing down to the river over the years and drifting happily to death. This is one fate.'

Benvy listened, puzzled, and began to feel a great weariness. 'I'm sorry. Do you mind if I sit? I'm so tired.'

'Sit, please,' replied the woman. She beckoned to a chair of stone immediately behind Benvy. It must have always been there, though Benvy hadn't noticed. She sat. It was quite comfortable, for a slab of rock.

'What do you mean, "one fate"?' she asked.

'I have seen the other too. The course you are on now. You are hard and strong and die like an oak, alone. Unloved.'

The woman began to pluck idly on the strings of her harp. The notes were disordered, but pleasing.

Benvy could not be sure she had heard correctly. The music coated her in warmth, caressing her. She stopped shivering. But the woman's words gnawed at her nevertheless.

'But that's silly. Lots of people love me!' she said sleepily, half to herself.

'Your friends *fear* you. You are a bully.'

'What? No! It's just joshing; they know that.' Benvy was slurring a little now.

'Your family *resent* you, because you were born a girl.'

'I'm tough because of my fam–' Benvy almost nodded off, but forced herself to concentrate. 'You try having an older brother! And parents that wish you were another son. And I'm not really ugly, am I? I could be pretty if I wanted. I ...'

The woman laughed and shifted her position. Her body was so lithe and shapely. Benvy had never seen anyone as perfect – even with the features of an animal.

'Pretty? No, dear. You are not pretty. A meadow is pretty. You are a bog.'

'Hey!' Benvy said, cross but drowsy. 'That's not ... I'm not ... Who the hell are you to say these things? What do you know about me?'

The woman *was* being very cruel. And yet Benvy still felt in awe of her, comfortable here in the warmth of the cave. *Maybe she's right, in a way.*

'I'm sorry, child, if I offend you further. It is not my intention. You seek the javelin of Taig McCormac. I would like you to have it. I am tired of guarding it. I will give it to you. First, there is a question. If you answer correctly, you can have your javelin. If your answer is wrong, you will die.'

Benvy was confused. She felt woozy. The room blurred in and out of focus while the notes trickled from the harp and swam in her head. 'Ask it then.' The words stumbled out of her.

'I am the truth – I see who you really are. You are a lie. You cannot accept the truth. My question is thus: do you wish to be true?'

'True?' Benvy slurred. 'What do you mean? Admit those things about my friends? My family? I ... I don't ...' *Maybe I am a liar,* she thought. *Maybe this woman is right and people are afraid of me; maybe my family do resent me and I just refuse to admit it. Maybe it's time for me to accept the real me.*

'What ... I mean ... I think so. I would like to be true.'

The woman grinned and ran her tongue along her teeth. They were long and sharp.

'I thought as much, child. You seem tired. Shall I play you a song?'

Music sounded like a great idea. Benvy was *so* tired, maybe a rest would do her good. And Taig's last words had been: *Listen to the music.*

'Yes, please.' She barely had the energy to form the words. Her eyelids were like lead.

The woman pulled the harp towards her and started to play with purpose. The sound was like wind in the leaves or waves on the sand. It was long grass, gurgling streams, birdsong, summer.

Benvy fought the urge to sleep, prising her eyes open with her fingers and looking blearily around her. The cavern walls seemed to writhe in time to the music, and her vision danced from thick blurriness to painful clarity. Flashes of light sparked like electric current behind her eyes, and it seemed the more she struggled, the sharper the bursts of pain. She tried to focus on the woman, willing the image to stop swaying, and battling wave upon wave of dizzy nausea, as the lights flared like fireworks just inches from her face.

For a moment she could see clearly, but it was all the more confusing, for dreams were starting to invade her waking vision. Where once the woman had been so distinctive, now she looked more than familiar. Thick, sandy hair tumbled onto strong shoulders. It framed a face that mirrored her own, but older, more graceful; more *proud*. Benvy realised it was herself, and felt a surge of hope that this was some vision of her future, until another wave of nausea took hold, and a fresh volley of lights assaulted her. It only eased when she allowed herself to slip into the warmth of the music and the heavy arms of sleep.

Benvy's eyes closed. But deep in the fog of her drowsiness something was addling her. A doubt about the woman was coaxing her out of slumber. Nothing this creature had said felt right. Nothing about *her* seemed real or true. She resisted the queasiness, ignored the sting of dazzling lights.

The fog cleared. '*You're* the lie!' Benvy roused herself and stood from the seat.

The woman stopped playing, and let out a seething hiss.

'You're the lie!' Benvy shouted again – fully alert now. 'All of those things you've said have been lies! I don't *wish* to be true: I'm Benvy Theodora Caddock. And that's as true as it gets!'

Before her, the woman began to change. Her cheeks fell like bags of pebbles; her eyelids swelled and then shrivelled around bloodshot eyes; her skin dried and cracked like baked mud. Her back hunched and her long hair, once black and glimmering, fell to the floor, while the tufts that remained, hardened into brittle white wires. She looked ancient.

'Go and be true to yourself then, Benvy Caddock. And have your prize.'

Propped against a nearby pillar was a javelin of red gold.

CHAPTER 11

A Secret's Bite

The inferno took the castle greedily, pulling it down into its white-hot belly, while Fergus and Sean watched from the forest, waiting for Goll. Sean had noticed a few figures escaping and running to the surrounding fields, and he worried that some may not have made it. Had anyone actually died as a result of their escape? He wasn't sure he could live with that, even though they had been more than happy to hang him. And he still could not quite believe what he had seen Goll do.

'And you say there are more of them – Old Ones – that can control the weather?' he asked Fergus.

'Not control as such, lad, no. They can call on it when they really need to. But yes, there are a few around,' Fergus replied. He was pinching the wound on his cheek to stem the blood flow. His beard was matted with it. In truth, he looked pretty haggard.

'Are you alright?' Sean asked.

'I'm grand. No need to ask again.'

'What did you say back there, to the captain I mean? Before you ...'

'I told him he was about to die,' said Fergus. For a moment his face was daubed with sadness. 'Thank you for stopping me.'

Dawn was arriving, brushing the horizon with purple as the blackened stump of the Norman stronghold spewed thick smoke into the sky. Around them the forest was waking up.

'Have you killed many people?' Sean asked after a while.

'Countless,' came the short response. It shocked the boy, but he tried not to show it.

'Do you think many died in that fire?'

'Only the ones who shouldn't have been there,' Fergus replied.

Sean didn't quite understand, but then something dawned on him: he had only seen Norman soldiers. He hadn't seen a single farmer or market trader or *normal* person. A sudden snap of a twig and a rustle of leaves behind them made him swerve. Emerging from the foliage was a throng of locals, all peasants; ten, twenty, thirty, fifty appeared through the thickets. They were all armed with whatever tools they could use to defend themselves. Goll was the last to appear.

'Well, Fergus McCormac, you always did have a knack

for turning up to the right fight at the right time!' he said jovially, clapping his hands on the giant's shoulders. 'Couldn't have done it without you, big man!'

He gestured to a nearby farmer, who approached and dropped their packs nervously at their feet, then hurried back to his people. Fergus and Sean were both shocked that their bags had been recovered, and shouted thanks after the retreating figure. The backpacks were singed black, but otherwise miraculously undamaged.

'You didn't do yourself any favours by getting locked up in the pillory, Goll!' Fergus said.

'Ach, you know yourself. I can't be pulling storms down whenever I feel like it. Anyways, the main thing is we hit them hard and these good folk are free. The struggle goes on, however.'

A voice from the throng said something in that Irish-like language, asking a question aimed at Fergus.

'Oh, he's real alright!' Goll laughed. 'In these parts the legend of Fergus the Mountain is very real indeed. And he'll be a great help in the struggle!'

'I'm afraid I can be of no further use, Goll,' said Fergus. 'We're only here by accident. And I hoped against hope that you might be around to help us find another gate. I thought I'd have to find a way to escape, and then search the land for you. The fact that you were there was nothing short of a miracle.'

'The girl?' Goll asked, suddenly grave.

'Aye.'

'Gods help us all. You'll be needing a few more miracles so. And you're taking this young fella to the Gomor first, I'm guessing?'

'I am.'

'Then may the gods help *you*, boy.'

Goll had brought them on a long and twisty path through the outskirts of the woods, avoiding the open plains where they might be seen. After a half a day's march, they had arrived at the foot of a wide and perfectly conical hill. At its summit, six imposing boulders stood, impossibly balanced on their narrowest points, each decorated with the now-familiar spirals. They circled a small mound of grass, which held three flat stones on one side. Between the stones was a deep and silent opening.

'Your gate,' Goll said. 'This should take you to where you need to go.'

Fergus and Sean thanked him, and Goll gave them each a long hug. As Sean was held in his musty arms, the druid whispered something in that old Irish, then added, 'A blessing of luck for you, Sean. I pray that it helps you. You will need all the help you can get.'

Fergus kneeled at the stones and began to hum, running his fingers along the pattern. Goll stood behind, arms raised, and joined in the droning. Clouds gathered, darkened and spilled heavy drops of rain on them to rolls of thunder. Fergus's wide finger left a trail of light behind it; the opening began to shine.

'On you go, lad,' Fergus instructed.

They emerged beside a murmuring stream, lined with tall reeds draped in mist. Around them, thrust from the earth, were steep mountains, coated in spiky grass of brown and amber and yellow. They loomed in and out of the thick grey haze like islands out at sea. Here and there, gushing streams cut down their sides, hurling themselves over sheer drops as waterfalls.

'Have you any food left, Sean?' Fergus was rooting through his own pack to see what he had.

'I have a couple of sandwiches, although I'd say they're gone off by now. They were egg.'

'You'll need something, anyway. Eat the bread. Take a drink from the stream. We'll need to get moving soon, and you'll need your strength.'

Fergus managed to find some big biscuits, wrapped in newspaper in the bottom of his bag. 'Here, have these. An old recipe. They'll help you along.'

'What about you?' Sean asked, genuinely concerned.

Fergus really wasn't looking his best, and the cut on his

cheek was leaking again.

'I'll be grand. It's you that needs it. No arguments: eat. I'll fill your flask.'

Sean didn't protest any further. He took a sandwich and scraped the pungent filling out, eating the bread hungrily. He took a piece of the biscuit and ate. It was good, like a full meal in just a mouthful.

'Wow, these are nice! What's in them?' he asked, spraying out bits of oat.

'Probably best you don't know. Here, drink.'

Sean took a long draft of the water. It was sensational, coursing down his throat; he could feel his body accepting it gratefully. After finishing the biscuit and taking another drink, they set off, heading up to higher ground and rounding the mountain they had emerged from. The going was tough as they climbed, picking their way through craggy rocks and slipping on the long, thick grasses. Sean felt energised by the food and water, but when Fergus suggested a break after a long march, he was hugely relieved.

From their new vantage point, the boy could see for the first time that they were close to the sea. The mountains fell down to it, their lower slopes disappearing into the metallic water at angles, forming bays and inlets where the water was calm. Further out, it boiled and thrashed, and Sean could make out the white lines of huge waves charging the coast. Ahead of them, the incline levelled out, dipped and rose again to another peak, as if two mountains were conjoined.

'We're not far now, lad. Just over that next hill is where you'll face your test,' Fergus said, grimly.

Sean knew there was no point in asking for any other information; he had already tried more than once. Fear squirmed again in his belly, but with false confidence he said: 'Fergus. So far I've been kidnapped in a forest, shown a magical vision, I lied to my mother, narrowly avoided arrest, had a crossbow aimed at my head and just managed not to get hung, instead welcoming fire and lightning just metres away from my face. Of all of those things, my mother is the most frightening. So I'm confident I can handle whatever is over that hill. And I don't know if you heard, but I'm good at tests.'

'I hope so, boy,' was all Fergus said.

When they had caught their breath and quenched their thirst, they lifted their bags onto tired shoulders and continued up the slope to where the mountain plateaued. The fog had thickened, so that they could only see a few metres around them. Ahead, the adjoining peak was a hulking grey phantom in the white. When the ground began to rise again, Fergus stopped.

'This is where I wait, Sean,' he said. 'On the other side of this hill there is a valley. In the valley is my hammer. The hammer belonged to my father, Cormac, and it has great power. But there is something else in that valley, Sean. There is death.'

Sean swallowed hard.

'Bring it back to me, lad,' Fergus said, patting the boy's shoulder. 'I believe you can.'

'No problem!' Sean replied, his over-confidence a thin mask. He was trembling. He gave a final worried smile, turned and set off up the incline.

From the top, Sean looked down a long but gentle descent of sharp rocks and auburn grasses to a valley mostly lost in the mist. There was total silence, except for a faint clicking sound that he guessed was some kind of bird. There was no sense in dallying; he picked his way among the stones. At the bottom, his range of vision did not improve much, and his glasses began to fog up, so that several times he had to take them off and wipe them on his shirt.

He made his way slowly along the valley floor, his eyes darting around him. He was only truly aware of the extent of his fear now. He was utterly petrified. He still couldn't see a great deal, and the landscape was unchanging, so that his sense of direction was skewed despite not having turned anywhere. The haphazard click click click persisted, growing a little louder as he went.

A few metres in front of him, he thought he could just make out the shadow of something in the cloud. Sean edged forward carefully, and soon there was no denying it:

something huge was in front of him and it moved, shuddering slightly. The noise was clearer now, and unmistakably coming from the spectre ahead. It was not just a click though; it was joined by something else, a kind of slobbering: squelching, snuffling, grunting. Like ... eating.

Now Sean was close enough to see. A colossal, gargantuan brute squatted before him: six metres tall even on his haunches. He was fat around the belly, but heavily muscled in the arms and shoulders. His body was covered in scars: thousands of them. They looked like nicks on his vast torso, but in reality were a metre or two long. Embedded here and there were weapons – swords, spears, arrows – all like splinters, and there for so long that they were nearly fossilised on the rough flesh. His head sported two very strange horns on the thick brow; instead of animal horns, they were like trees with clutches of oblong red leaves. Greasy wild hair fell around pointy ears.

In the monster's vast hands, tipped with long grey nails, he held the carcass of a huge male elk. He was gorging himself on it, the bones clicking and snapping between his blood-soaked teeth. The animal's once noble head, crowned with wide antlers, hung slack between the ogre's fingers, the eyes rolled back to the whites and jaw agape.

Sean had not been noticed yet. He thought about running, but then, inexplicably, his mouth opened and he said, 'Excuse me.'

The ogre looked up from its meal instantly, turning its head left and right with the poor elk still clamped in his jaws.

'Down here!' Sean shouted. He could not believe himself. The creature looked down at him, its dark eyes boring into his. It let the carcass drop; blood slid down its chin in heavy drops. For a moment there was utter silence. Then the ogre rose to its feet, opened its mouth wide and bellowed long and hard into Sean's face. The boy's ears popped and rang; his cheeks flapped as if he was in a wind tunnel. He fell backwards, his glasses coated in blood and green spittle.

Scuttling desperately to his feet, he found he could see nothing around him, but he realised he was not being eaten, yet. Sean wiped away the thick grease from his glasses and looked ahead. The ogre was standing back a few feet from him. It looked confused, even a little *frightened*.

It seemed to be staring at something by Sean's feet. Sean looked to the ground beside him and saw his bag. It had fallen when he was knocked back, and spilled its contents. The monster kept glancing between the bag and the boy while shuffling backwards.

This makes no sense, Sean thought. Then, once again, he did something completely independently of his own will (which wanted him to run): he leaned down and picked up one of his books from the wet grass. It was the hardcover he had bought in the Ailwee Caves: *Symbols in Stone: Celtic Carvings of Ancient Ireland*. The cover sported a photograph of stones around an ancient burial mound, each coated in spirals. The monster flinched, holding up a huge arm as if to defend itself from a blow. Sean held the book up higher and the ogre shuffled back, visibly cowed. Sean started to understand.

'Eh ... foul beast!' he shouted, 'I am the great ... uh ... the great ... Zed! Yes, I am Zed the Powerful! Look on my works, ye mighty, and despair!' He waved the book threateningly. The monster groaned and turned in a circle, as if searching for an escape.

'This is my book of spells! And now ... uh,' Sean was really thinking on his feet here. *Keep going*, said an inner voice. 'And now, I shall read from it and you will be killed!'

The ogre was beginning to look completely confused. It frowned, snuffled out a low growl and pounded its great fist on the earth. Sean took a step backwards, tripped over his bag and fell onto his backside. The creature slammed a fist into the ground again and stepped closer. It was not as afraid as Sean had hoped.

He held up the book again and with his free hand groped on the ground around him. He found his other book – his fantasy paperback. He held it aloft for the goliath to see, and when the ogre noticed the image of swords and lightning on the cover, with the foil catching the grey light just enough to shimmer slightly, it roared into the air and leaped back again. Getting to his feet and keeping the shiny paperback aloft, Sean opened a random page of the *Symbols in Stone* hardback and started to read:

'Iron Age carved head.' He waved the book around his head for effect, and stepped towards the cowering beast. 'Found in 1927 in the area of Oristown, County Meath, this stone figure is thought to portray the god Dagda.'

The ogre began to weep.

It fell to its knees and bowed its head, scratching the ground around itself, pulling up soil and rock, and beating itself around the shoulders with fistfuls of earth. It glanced up once and then curled up, tucking its face into its chest. It peeked out from between its fingers, then reached behind its back and produced a huge hammer, easily the height of the boy and probably twice his weight. The monster set it down at his feet, whining. The shaft was bound in leather; the head was moulded to the shape of a fist.

When Fergus saw the boy appear over the crest of the hill, his heart leapt for joy, and then fell again when he could not see the hammer. He hurried to meet him.

'No weapon, lad?' he asked, sadly. 'You are alive at least.'

Sean whistled.

The ground shook, and the goliath stomped out of the mist. It grumbled at Fergus, set the hammer down and then turned. Roaring once, it slipped back into the fog. The bellow echoed through the mountains and out onto the cold ocean.

Consciousness came back to Ayla slowly, in surges of dull pain and nausea. When she opened her eyes, she could just make out a thin beam of brilliant light shimmying before her. She groaned and squinted, and the blurriness abated slightly. At least three of the goblin creatures were scurrying around her, pulling parts of the contraption across and down expertly. It shunted and clicked noisily as they worked, the wooden parts sliding and lifting, folding the string of light into a weave and carrying it off somewhere to her left. When they noticed her wake, they cackled and said:

'Not long now, Princess Piglet! The loom works quickly!'

Ayla focused on the light. It was a taut beam, painfully bright, and it pointed directly down onto her body. It danced from left to right and back again, burning her where it touched. It was focused on her right arm now, biting sharply into the flesh at the elbow joint.

She raised her head weakly to see better, and screamed in horror. Below the elbow, her lower arm was transformed.

The skin was charred: blacker than black. Her hand was long and crooked, with gnarled, claw-like fingers, curling up into a fist. Frantically she tried to lift her head higher again, to inspect the rest of her body, and cried out again at the sight of her right leg: it too was changed. It was thin and bent, with a long foot and grasping toes. The pitch-black-coloured skin extended to her hip and up to the lower ribs.

'What are you doing to me?' she wailed.

The red roots of the king's face appeared far above her, then descended, crimson sparks falling from his eyes and mouth. The heat stung her entire body. He smelled of rotten earth.

'LOOK!'

The voice boomed like a piece of a cliff crashing into the sea. His hand of tangled vines pointed to her right.

Ayla looked. From the machinations of the loom a tapestry of light emerged and, guided by teams of goblins, trailed across the great hall and into the wretched form that hung from the wall. The form was nearly whole now; Ayla could see the shapes of two arms hanging down on either side of an open torso, though they still draped lifelessly. Goblins threaded the weave among the roots, and as they worked, Ayla saw it twitch violently. Whatever she was, she was beginning to stir.

The king spoke again.

'Long have we searched for you.'

Ayla looked back at him, horrified.

'Many times we thought we had found you.'

The goblins howled.

'Now our daughter has returned to us, and my love can be whole again.'

Finny, Benvy and Sean were hugging feverishly, none of them willing to break the embrace. At last, Benvy pushed them off in mock disgust. They laughed and hugged again.

'I never thought I'd see you again!' Finny shouted.

'I never thought I'd see anything again!' Benvy replied, tousling his hair.

Lann and Fergus stood on a ridge a few metres away, deep in conversation. Taig sat on a boulder alone. They were on a flat plain of limestone rock, which cracked into deep fissures. The landscape rolled away around them into round hills, with only splashes of green where stubborn plants grew between the slabs. The sky was ashen, and laden with fat clouds. The brothers beckoned the three friends over to them.

'We have to set off. Night will fall soon,' announced Lann. 'We have only an hour or so of a march, but we will be moving quickly. If you have any food and water left, I suggest you take it now.'

Sean shared some biscuit among them, and they wolfed it down gratefully. They shared their flasks too, and lifted their bags onto each others' backs.

Lann and Fergus started off ahead of them, heading across the plain to a cluster of small mountains. Taig was still sitting in the distance, on his boulder. The friends looked at each other, sharing the same expression of concern.

'They don't look well,' Sean said. 'Fergus has been struggling for a while.'

'They look older,' added Finny. 'And what's up with Taig, Benv?'

'I'm not sure,' she replied. 'He's been in a right grump since I got the javelin. I don't think he feels so good.'

They watched the youngest brother lift himself heavily from his seat and trudge off in the direction of the mountains.

'Well, who's going to go first?' asked Finny.

'Allow me,' Sean said quickly, and began to recount his tale in great detail as they walked.

By the time they arrived at the mountains, each had had a chance to tell their story. They had gasped in astonishment at each others' accounts, still finding their situation hard to believe. They could only imagine what lay ahead of them now. But all three admitted to feeling more ready for whatever was thrown at them. They just wanted to find Ayla.

Fergus and Lann did not stop, continuing on a rough path between the flanks of the rocky mountains. It grew colder with every step, and the going was difficult. Wide cracks had to be crossed; the ground was ridged and hard on their feet.

When they began the climb up the tallest of the peaks, they saw no more tufts of sturdy grass, nor heard any trickles of lively streams. They each got the unpleasant sense that they were going to a place where even the most determined life had no foothold. This place was dead – a purgatory of hard, unending limestone.

Taig lagged far behind for the whole of the unceasing climb, but every time Benvy checked, he was still there at least, hauling himself slowly up.

At the top, it was bitingly cold, despite there being no hint of a breeze. Ahead of them, Lann and Fergus had stopped and gestured down to the other side.

A craggy escarpment tumbled down to a deep-set canyon. While the land around them had been sterile and colourless, this valley was worse still. It was harsh – cruel even. The three friends each had a strong distaste for going anywhere near it.

In the centre of the cold vale was a single hawthorn tree. It thrust its sharp branches out at an angle from the stones at its base, clawing at the sky with bark the colour of fresh blood. The two brothers began the descent without saying anything. There was no choice but to follow them.

They stood around the tree, shivering. It took Taig a long time to catch up with them, and no one spoke or even looked at each other as they waited. When the fair-headed giant arrived, he was shockingly pale. His taut skin sagged and his blond hair had whitened and thinned. Benvy went to him, but he waved her away, crossly. His two older brothers were themselves weakened and sickly, but they stared at the youngest with strange expressions.

'I don't understand,' Taig said meekly. 'I don't understand why this is happening. This shouldn't be happening to me.'

'You knew the price, brother,' Fergus said, though confusion was etched on his face.

'He did not think he would have to pay it,' said Lann, grimly. 'He thought he'd struck a deal.'

The friends looked at each other and then to the brothers.

'Taig? What deal?' Benvy asked as tears welled up.

The youngest brother looked at her, and then at Lann and Fergus.

'I thought they would all fail!' he shouted, and then coughed harshly. A drop of blood hit the ground at his feet.

'So, it *was* you,' said Lann. 'You gave Ayla to them.'

Fergus took a step towards him, but was stopped by the hand of his older brother.

'Yes, I gave her to them! What is she to us but a *curse!*' Taig spat, hacking up more blood. 'I knew we could go home. *Our* home! And so I used that wench Deirdre to help me to contact them. I told them where she was. And I was promised ...'

A fit of coughing cut him off.

'*You little* ...!' Fergus tried again to rush him, but was held firmly by Lann, who pulled the great red head towards him and whispered something. Fergus nodded angrily. They both stooped at the foot of the hawthorn tree, and began to hum.

They began running their fingers along unseen patterns in the stones at the base of the tree, and light shone from their fingertips. There was a heavy *boooom!* as the ground split with a wide yawn. Thick, warm air rushed out of the hole.

'Go!' Lann ordered the friends. Fergus handed them each their weapon, and gave Sean a long look.

'It is heavy, lad. But you are strong,' Lann said, pushing the boy towards the opening.

When the three had entered the hollow, they looked back. They each shouted to the uncles to hurry, but in a second the ground shut and they were alone in the dark.

CHAPTER 12

A Battle Below

The three friends now found themselves trapped deep beneath the earth. The ceiling was low in the tight, musty passageway. The walls were a mass of thick, red roots that surfaced from mud and stone, and sank again like the backs of sea serpents. They coiled on the ground, leaving barely any flat surface on which to stand. The three did not move for a few minutes. They hunched quietly in the inky blackness, close to tears.

Sean spoke first: 'How could he do it? How could he betray her like that?'

For a while there was silence again, none of them knowing what to say, until Finny made a decision. 'We'll have to move sooner or later. There seems to be only one way to go – down.'

Feeling with his feet and hands, Finny led the way, with

Sean holding his rucksack for safety and Benvy holding
Sean's. They were completely blind in the dark, so Finny
made slow progress, with his hand held out in front. While
his sword was deceptively light, and Benvy's javelin perfectly balanced, they were cumbersome and awkward, and
they had to find a way to carry them without taking out
an eye or worse.

Sean could barely lift Fergus's huge hammer. They had
to run it through the flap on his rucksack, and he bore
the weight painfully on his back as best he could. They
shuffled on, bent over under the low roof, as the path sank
further down into the bowels of the earth. It was Sean
who noticed it first.

'Finny, your sword!'

'What?' Finny asked, holding the blade up. It was odd;
he didn't know what he was looking for at first, but he
knew something was different. And then it dawned on
him: he could see the weapon as clearly as in daylight,
despite being in total darkness. It even gave off a dim light.

'Uh, Sean. Have a look at that big hammer of yours,' he
said. 'Benvy, your javelin is at it too!'

Benvy said nothing; she was trying hard not to give in
to tears.

Sensing Benvy's deep upset, Finny said, 'Benvy, we have
to ...'

'I know, I know. I just can't help ...' she rubbed her eyes

and breathed in to compose herself. 'He was so nice to me. The whole way, up until the cave. And his last words to me were "Listen to the music". I thought I must have misheard him, but now ... He wanted me to fail. He wanted me to ... *die*. I just ...'

'I know it hurts, Benv',' said Sean, 'but we can't think about it now. He's out there and we're in here. We have to find Ayla and get her out. That's all we can think about.'

Benvy nodded, wiping her eyes with her sleeve again.

'Right, I'm fine. Let's go get Ayla and get the hell out of here.'

They continued into the shadows.

The light from their weapons was only very slight, but it was enough to show their immediate surroundings at least. The tunnel was still low and hot, the walls dry and rough, but after twenty minutes of walking they began to notice patterns on the wall. More and more of them appeared as they went: intricate carvings woven together in complex arrangements. Then they noticed the first carved head, with its sharp ears and wide, round eyes. More and more of these appeared, so that the design became more frightening. They decided together not to pay them any more attention. After a time, the tunnel widened a bit, and they were able to stand up straight for the first time. A little further down, they encountered their first branch in the passageway.

'Well, do we keep going or try this way?' Sean asked.

No one had an answer.

'We could split?' suggested Finny. No one liked this idea, but he persisted. 'Look, we don't know where to go. We could get lost forever down here. If we split up, at least one of us has a chance of finding her.'

They couldn't argue with that logic. Finny volunteered to take the new passage. Benvy and Sean would continue on.

'If you get into trouble ...'

'I'll be fine, lads,' he said, and left.

As soon as Sean and Benvy saw the light in the tunnel ahead, they stopped dead in their tracks and pressed themselves to the wall. Torchlight was coming from around a corner up ahead, where the ceiling rose suddenly tall and the passage widened into a broad chamber. They listened for a while, holding their breath, and then edged forward as carefully as they could.

Benvy risked a peek, slowly moving one eye just past the corner. Another long corridor stretched out ahead, lit by several small torches. Apart from them, it was empty. At the far end was a small hole, just big enough for a person to fit through.

'The coast is clear,' she said. 'Come on.'

They crept silently along the passage to the hole. Inside was blackness.

'Hang on a sec',' said Sean, and fetched one of the torches from the wall. He held it down to the opening and looked inside.

'It's just a tiny room,' he said. 'No doorways or anything. Not even big enough to stand in.'

Benvy bent down to see for herself. He was right; there was nothing to it – just a pit, like a badger might live in. The only thing of note was a collection of broken pottery shards scattered on the floor at the far end.

'Hang on,' she said, taking the torch from Sean. She pushed through the hole and held the flame to the ground. There was something there among the shards, small and black just like them, but of a different shape. It caught her eye, half-buried in the loose muck. She lifted it and blew the dust off.

'It's her phone, Sean!' she said. 'Dead as a doornail though.'

'We must be close,' he said, pulling her out.

Finny was utterly lost. He had taken the new passageway for a good twenty minutes before encountering a series of new tunnels, shooting off in all directions. Eventually, his route came to a dead end, and he had no choice but to pick one. He chose the archway closest to him for want of a better option, and followed it down and down, veering left and right, then climbing, then falling further. Twice he came to forks and decided on the wider of the two, only to find himself crawling on hands and knees through airless arteries of dust.

Finny came to a point where the path rose steeply and he hauled himself up, arriving into a wider space at last. The air was only slightly less stale here, and he took a moment to rest on the ground. He didn't allow himself long. *Come on Finnegan*, he told himself and got to his feet. At least here he could stand to his full height. Holding the sword out, he could see that the walls were decorated with the same horrible carvings they had seen before.

The chamber was wide, and he sighed at the sight of yet more passageways. The other end was in darkness, but as he approached slowly he could make out a large crack in the wall ahead, and then noticed that he could continue past it, around a corner. He rounded it into another sizeable room, where the walls held two extinguished torches, still smoking. Finny moved forward and then stopped. His form was suddenly cast in shadow in front of him, as a light appeared from nowhere behind. He spun around and gasped: two white orbs like headlights shone on him. Below them, a mouth of burning coals opened and seethed at him. Before he could do anything, he was struck across the face by a sharp claw. He fell to the ground unconscious, his torn cheek oozing blood.

There was nowhere else to go but back. Benvy and Sean made their way to the point where they had separated with Finny, more frustrated with every step. After the high of discovering Ayla's phone, it now seemed like they were starting all over again. But with no other choice, they pushed on down Finny's tunnel until they came to a collection of passageways.

'We need to take the first left,' Sean said.

'What? Why? Are you sure?'

'I'm sure. We'll be going back in the right direction then at least.'

Sean lead the way and Benvy followed, impressed by his confidence.

'Sean,' she began, as they ducked under low hanging rocks.

'Yeah?'

'If we don't make it out of this ...'

'We'll make it.'

'No, but look, *if we don't* ... I want you to know ...' she hesitated.

'Know what?' He had stopped.

'Um ... know that you'll always be ...' she swallowed. 'You'll always be a *total* nerdlinger.'

Silently, she berated herself for being such a chicken.

'Yeah, yeah,' he said and started to move again. 'You'll always be my best nerdlinger too, Benvy Caddock.'

She smiled and followed him down the tunnel.

After a series of tight turns and drops, they emerged at last to a wide cavity. It was well lit, and they entered carefully, but they found it empty. To the right, the way disappeared back into blackness; straight ahead was the beginning of another passage. It was the sight to their left, however, that made them gasp.

It was a gigantic door, adorned with a relief that was both incredible and terrifying in equal measure. It featured thousands of gremlin-like creatures – the same ones that decorated the wall murals throughout the warren of tunnels. They were all writhing on top of one another and pointing up. At the top, there was a tree, from which spilled a mess of endlessly long roots, flowing down the face of the door and ending at the goblins' long fingers. From the other side, noise filtered through, too muffled to discern, but loud enough that they knew this was, in all likelihood, where they would find Ayla.

'What do we do now?' Benvy asked. 'I'm guessing we don't just knock! And where the hell is Finny? I thought we would have found him by now. I hope he's okay!'

'Let's go straight ahead,' replied Sean, his authority growing. 'We'll see if there's another way in to whatever is behind that door.'

They crossed the wide chamber as quickly as they could, and hurried under the low vault of the adjacent passage. It narrowed again to little more than a crawlspace, but the noise didn't abate, and so they were sure they had made the right decision. Eventually, they pushed through, into another large hollow. Sean waved the weakening torch around to inspect. At the far end, there was a pool of black water. Just at its edge, half-submerged, was the grizzly sight of a mutilated carcass – that of a massive toad. It had been stripped to the bare skeleton but for its large head, which remained, dead-eyed, a fat tongue spilling from its mouth.

'Gross!' said Benvy.

'There's another door.' Sean was pointing to another opening directly across from the one they had come through.

They climbed up to it, but found little more than a burrow. The noise was clearly close now, and so they helped each other in and crawled, pushing their burdensome weapons in front of them. Ahead was light, and the chilling sound of baying crowds: shriek upon shriek, howl upon howl. They forced their way along to its source.

They emerged on a ledge, where there was just enough room to lie side by side on their stomachs. Slack-jawed, neither could speak. From their perch they gazed upon the immense hall with its mammoth pillars. The broiling black of thousands of goblins, swarming over each other, eyes like full moons and red mouths squealing, was like looking into hell. To the right, the great hall stretched away, impossibly high and wide, ending in the most dizzying sight of all. On a towering stone throne was the form of a bearded man, thirty metres tall, made entirely of roots. At his feet stood a wooden machine, like an old catapult, but it was almost impossible to make out more.

Then Benvy realised she could make out a familiar figure. She shouted, '*Finny!*' And with that, she leaned too far over the rocky lip. She fell.

Sean only hesitated for a second. He took the hammer up into both fists, stood on the edge of the tiny platform and leaped, roaring, into the throng. It was a huge jump, out and over the mass of black creatures, between the pillars and down, down, down. As he dropped, he raised his weapon over his head, and as the ground rushed up towards him he brought it down to fall upon the stone floor.

It cracked the earth like an eggshell, hurling the shrapnel

of thick stone into the air around him. A wave of muck and rock rushed off in a circle around him, carried on a disc of blazing blue light. It smashed through the swarm, pitching the creatures into the air in their hundreds. Cracks rushed up the four nearest pillars like snakes, and the roof rained dust in blinding swathes. The whole hall shook violently, as if it was being throttled.

Sean coughed out a cloud of dry muck, and took his hands from the shaft of the hammer. His glasses were coated in grime; he wiped them on his shirt, but the lens that had been cracked was now smashed. He looked around him, then down at his legs. He was in one piece at least. The hammer was buried fast, halfway into a massive slab of granite; there was no removing it. Around him was a thick fog of dirt, and pieces of the hall still slipped and crashed to the ground. There was no other movement.

'*Benvy!*' he yelled, and again, '*Benvyyy!*'

He ran over to where he guessed she had fallen, and there she was, out cold. There were no goblins around her. A fresh trickle of blood ran from her forehead; in her right hand, she still clenched the javelin. Sean rushed to her side and took her head in his lap, gently slapping her face and begging her to wake up.

'Benvy, please! Please wake up!' he pleaded. He wiped the blood from her head, and saw that it was only a scratch. Her eyes opened, and blinked, darting around in confusion.

'Thank God!' he shouted. 'I thought I'd killed you!'

'What ... What the hell?' Benvy was still confused. Then she jolted up. 'Finny! Sean, I saw Finny. He's here! They have him!'

From behind the smog of debris, there was a deafening roar and a blast of searing heat. The two hurried to their feet and looked into each other's eyes. Without saying anything, they nodded and ran in the direction of the roar, as the cloud began to dissipate.

Around them, hordes of goblins were getting to their feet, lamp-like eyes sending beams into the dust like spot-lights. Ahead, the monstrous form of the king was pull-ing great chunks of stone from its legs: he was half lying between the two split sides of his broken throne. In front of him, the wooden platform had been damaged, but remained working, and they could see the strange cloth of light flowing out from it and over into the shadowy eaves.

Directly in front of them, the body of Finny was limp, in the grip of a dozen creatures. They were pulling at him and thrashing him, even though he was unconscious. As they ran, Sean and Benvy could see their friend was bloodied and badly beaten.

All around them, the black things were rising to their feet and beginning the chase. The monstrous king had freed himself, and now rose with a bellow of fire. Benvy raised the javelin over her head, and threw it with every ounce of strength she possessed.

It tore through the air in a blaze of white and a head-bursting scream. The whole hall was bathed in its blinding glow as it shot like a hot bullet straight into the chest of the king. To either side, creatures fell to the ground, with bleeding ears, yelping and clawing at their own eyes, howling in pain. The group that held Finny rolled away in blind agony, leaving him slumped on the ground. His two friends rushed to his side and lifted him up. He was badly cut; his face, torso, arms and legs were shredded, his clothes sodden with blood.

'Wake *up*!' they shouted at their friend, frantically checking to see if any of his cuts were fatal.

'Please, Finny!' they begged, 'Please, just wake up!'

From what they could see, the wounds were deep, but he wouldn't bleed to death.

He groaned and spat out a glob of blood.

'Ayla ...' was the first thing he said.

'Yes! Finny! Up you get now! You're hurt, but we can get you out of here!' Benvy shouted.

'Ayla ...' he repeated.

'We don't know where she is!' Benvy said, 'We need to get out of here and figure out what to do. We need to get you out and see if we can patch ...'

Sean put a hand on her arm.

'There's no getting out of here without her,' he said. 'We

may as well die trying.'

Benvy couldn't reply. Her mouth had dried, and the words were stuck. But she knew Sean was right.

Over the surrounding rubble, goblins were pouring, scratching at each other to get to them first. Then another deafening, thunderous roar came from behind the platform. The king had risen to his feet. They could see a burning hole in his chest where the javelin had entered, but the singed wound seemed to have had little effect. His eyes widened, red infernos in the veil of dust.

'KILL!'

The voice gripped their ears in fists of sound. They covered them and squeezed their eyes shut against the pain. The goblins were nearly upon them.

CHAPTER 13

A Song of Goodbye

When the creatures were close enough to pounce, Sean threw himself in front of Benvy, ordering her to stay behind. She wrenched him back with one hand, and held him there with the other.

'Finny!' she yelled above their baying, 'Your sword! You have to get to Ayla!'

Finny looked around frantically for the weapon, but it wasn't on the ground.

'Go!' his two friends shouted in unison, readying themselves for a fight to the death, their backs to each other.

Finny put a first foot on the wooden structure. Behind him he heard the slavering growls of the goblins as they leaped onto his friends; he heard Benvy and Sean shouting in the fray, each ordering the other to save themselves. But he didn't turn to look. He climbed, wincing in pain and bleeding heavily.

At the top, the machine was busy, shunting left and right, pulling a thread of bright light from something unseen behind part of the structure, and weaving it into a thick tapestry. It was damaged from the shockwave of Sean's hammer. It slouched now where one of its huge wheels had snapped off the axle. On the same side, the granite had split and part of it had fallen to the ground. Motionless black arms and legs could be seen under the fallen slab. Three of the goblins had rushed to replace their fallen comrades, and worked feverishly at the loom, pulling the thick weave and passing it on to others on the ground below.

They had not yet seen Finny. He pulled himself painfully up over the top of the whole structure, moved behind the upright frame and ducked underneath the jostling beams. Then he had his first piece of luck: the sword was leaning against a balustrade, right by the feet of the goblin workers. He summoned his strength and went for it.

In four long leaps, Finny made it to the weapon, grabbed it and sidestepped the first assailant. Once again, just as in the dim basin where he faced the changeling, he imagined himself in a match. *They're just other players*, he convinced himself through the fear. He ducked the next as it swung a haggard claw at his head, and in one movement struck the third on the head with the flat of the blade.

His own wounds opened wider, and his body howled

at him to stop, but he ignored it, spinning around to jump a low swipe, and pushed forward with a shoulder into another goblin, knocking it over the side. His last deft turn put him beside the third goblin as it went for him again. He knocked its claw away with his hand and swung at it with the sword. This time he used the edge: the blade went through the creature's arm like it was butter, and the thing wailed and jumped over the side, the severed arm twitching angrily by Finny's feet. The whole structure wobbled as more goblins scaled it. He turned, searching for an escape, and saw his friend.

Ayla was held up at an angle, arms and legs strapped in leather and bound in chains. From her neck, the glimmering thread protruded up into the loom, unravelling her. Only her face and one arm remained; the rest was night-black and contorted. She was turning into one of them.

'Ayla!' he shouted, but his cry was lost in the thunderclap of the king's red-hot bellow.

The vast king towered over them, spitting ash and firefly sparks. The vines of his arm squirmed and slid together as he reached down and knocked Finny into the air. He landed hard against a pillar and slumped to the ground. The boy's wounds were leaking, hot and wet on his cheek and arms. His vision blurred and everything around him tilted. He felt sick as he tried to get to his feet, and toppled over on to his head, rolling on the floor. Still he tried to lift himself, but his legs had turned to boneless lumps.

Finny could hear the crashing stomps as the gargantuan king approached again; he could just make out the jostling herds of goblins, holding each other back and cackling, slapping their hands on the floor like frenzied apes, bloodthirsty and ravenous for his death at the hands of their master.

He focused on the fabric of light that stretched over his head, and followed its course between the pillars. The stomps grew closer as he saw the wretched shape of the half-finished root-woman dangling from the wall, where the weave knitted itself into her: arms, chest, stomach and the frightful head, whose face tugged at the wall to be free, and screamed with the sound of a hundred banshees.

Finny staggered like a drunk as the first blow came down on the ground beside him, casting him into the air like a rag doll. Again he pulled himself up, forcing the sick back down into his stomach, sticking his chin out and holding the sword up weakly. Finny tried to shout something, but he had no strength. The red root king brought its fist down again in a huge detonation, right beside the boy, knocking him back to the rubble – he was so close to death, he could feel its cold clutch.

'DIE!'

The shock of the king's growl split Finny's ears and wrenched at his brain, and for a second he was lost. He let the dark curtains of unconsciousness close around him, taking sad comfort in the slow slide to oblivion. And suddenly he was in the woods – in Coleman's, in their little place. And he was angry, swinging his hurley at the leaves, spitting out every bad word he knew and cursing his life. And Ayla was there, saying nothing, letting him do it. And when he tired and slumped to the ground, she put her arm around him. She lifted his face by the chin, looked at him with those vivid-green eyes boring in ... and she said, 'You'll always have me.'

And he woke.

He placed the point of the blade on the ground, and hoisted himself up to standing. The demon king stood before him, about fifty metres away, vast and cruel and grinning. The hordes encircled him, whooping and crying out for him to die. The vile figure on the wall strained at her own body, pulling the thread into herself, the fire in her eyes and mouth coming alive – indicating that the process was nearly complete. It was the evil queen, Maeve, Finny knew now. And only Ayla's death would set her free.

He held the sword by his waist, one hand on the handle and the other on the end of the blade, just as he would his hurley before a free. He parted his legs to steady his stance, sidelong to his target. And he whispered to the weapon, 'Let's see what you can do then!'

He brought the sword up behind his head, took a few

steps forward and swung. The weapon sang, slicing the air and shining effervescent blue. As it travelled, the blue grew longer, an extension of the blade – ten metres, twenty, thirty. It bit into the roots of the king's crown, severing them cleanly – as if there was nothing there at all. Finny spun on his feet, the light retracting as he brought the sword down, in the same movement, onto the weave. The threads disintegrated.

Finny looked to the king. The monstrous mangle of roots gazed back, its face contorted into a look of shock. The behemoth could only watch as the weave–light dimmed and went out. It saw its lover writhe, unfinished, on the wall. It regarded Finny, and tried to reach out a hand, but the flames in its eyes and mouth dimmed and then died out. The king crashed to the floor in an explosion of wood and dust, the brittle roots snapping as they fell.

The only sound now was the desperate wailing of the queen, and though that pierced like a pin in his ears, Finny realised she could not move from the wall. The goblins were silent and motionless. They didn't rush the boy or attack, or even howl at him; they just stood and stared with those round, pale eyes.

Finny half-limped, half-ran to the loom and, with great effort, climbed the steps to Ayla, or what was left of her. He had stopped the thread just as it reached her chin. Nearly all of her was transformed, and she didn't move. He cut the bonds and lifted her onto his shoulder. Where the skin was black she was ice-cold, but her cheek felt warm against his. He made his way down slowly, fighting the urge to collapse. Behind the loom, where he had last seen his friends, he found Benvy, hunched over an unconscious Sean, weeping. Both of them were covered in cuts.

'Finny! You did it!' Benvy said, trying, but failing, to smile. 'I missed the whole thing; just woke up. Is Ayla okay?'

And then she saw the slumped figure in his arms, half-transformed, with those jagged goblin limbs.

'Oh Finny! She's ...'

'She's turning into one of them. We have to go, Benv'. These things are going to let us, I think. But I don't know how long that will last. Is Sean okay?'

'He wouldn't fight for himself,' she lamented. 'The big eejit kept fighting them off me. He's hurt badly, Finny. He won't wake up.'

Sean's face was coated in dark blood, his eyes bound shut where it had dried over them.

'Let's go.'

Sean coughed and groaned, a trickle of blood snaking down his chin.

'Oh, thank God!' shouted Benvy. 'Shush, don't talk. Can you walk at all?'

Sean could only answer with a pained moan, but did his best to get to his feet with her help. He was still heavy, and she almost collapsed, but righted herself and nodded to Finny to follow. It was only as they walked that they noticed all of the goblins slinking away into the shadows under the broken pillars.

Benvy had a good idea of how to get out. Taking a torch from the wall with her free hand, she led them through the labyrinth. The caterwauling of the half-queen haunted them as they struggled through the undulating passages, but it lessened with distance, and by the time they turned left at the last junction, it was only the echoes that reached them. They climbed on, their hearts fluttering as they recognised the tunnel they had first come to, and knew that they were at the gate. Before they could wonder at how to open it, the earth parted before them and they blocked their eyes against the warm, wet daylight.

◎ ◎ ◎

The three friends did not have time to talk, or to allow their stinging eyes to adjust. They felt themselves dragged out of the hole by huge hands, and set down on the wet stone to suck in lungfuls of air. They could hear Lann and Fergus speaking, but they allowed themselves another minute to breathe and for their day-blind eyes to grow used to the outside. When at last they could look, they were shocked at the sight of all three giant brothers.

Gone were the broad shoulders and tree-trunk arms. Gone was the hair of black, red and blond. All their features were lost to age, drained and shrivelled and cracked. Heavy bags swung under yellowed eyes. Their cheeks had sunk and sagged. Their backs were hunched, the spines prodding through white, translucent skin. Taig looked the worst; he was toothless and frail, barely able to lift his head. He sat alone.

'You're ...' Finny started.

'We're dying, lad,' the old shell of Lann said. 'The price of returning home.'

Fergus did not speak. He was arranging Ayla's limp body among a circle of small stones. To see the once-mighty Fergus struggle with the weight, where once he could have lifted her with one finger, was a sad sight. He was muttering curses under his wispy white beard, and coughed in a dry hack from his failing lungs.

'Can you save her?' Finny asked. His own wounds were grievous, and he couldn't get up. 'Can you save Ayla?'

'We can,' Lann answered.

Bleak clouds had gathered, and the atmosphere was heavy. Finny noticed the hawthorn tree had wilted to a charcoal stump like a grasping hand. His wounds throbbed. Sean had slipped into unconsciousness again, and Benvy was trying to wake him, with no luck.

Fergus stood over them. He kneeled slowly down beside

Sean and placed a tender hand on the boy's forehead. While Fergus's body was frail, draped over like a brittle skeleton, his hands had not changed – they were still heavy and thickset.

'It looks like you could do with some healing your-selves,' Fergus said, his own gash now a scar lost among the wrinkles. 'We can help. Have faith.'

Benvy thanked him, but nodded to Taig.

'Why is *he* still here?' she asked scornfully.

'He is here to amend,' Fergus replied. 'He's our brother, Benvy. You should forgive him.'

She looked at him again.

'I don't think I can.'

◎ ◎ ◎

It was dusk when the uncles had finished their preparations. They kneeled beside Ayla's prone body inside the ring of round stones, which were piled into a low wall. Finny, Benvy and Sean lay behind them, weak and tired. A roll of thunder grumbled in the brooding clouds and a few drops of rain fell. The three brothers were silent for a long while, each with his head bowed and eyes closed. They seemed so feeble now, like the discarded skins of once-great men. With another smack of thunder, they started to sing.

The harmonies wove together in cavern-deep bass; the

notes were mournful and achingly beautiful. The lyrics swooped and thrummed and danced together, moulded into ancient Irish words by the withered mouths. As they sang, each opened his shirt. On their chests were old, deep scars in the shape of a spiral. They each placed a finger at the start and traced the lumpy tissue to the centre, leaving a blaze of white where it went. When they reached the middle, they pulled the light out of their chests in thick threads.

The notes wavered for just a moment, then grew louder as the clouds boomed in unison with their fathomless voices. They placed the threads on Ayla's chest and opened their eyes: they were brilliant white. The rain fell around them, but not a drop touched their bodies. The light sank into her as they pulled more and more out of themselves. The song dipped and soared, like a river underground. The black on her skin retreated, her true form gradually returning.

Taig reached a hand back and placed it on Benvy's foot. Fergus did the same, resting his on Sean. Lann found Finny's hand and held it. The healing glow coursed through them all, and their wounds faded, leaving fresh skin. It felt like being plunged into an icy pool on a hot day. The three voices joined in one low note while the gusts tugged at their clothes, their beards and hair. Ayla was whole again and her eyes blinked, awake. She looked around her and saw her uncles, recognising them despite their ageing, and she wept hot tears.

'Goodbye, Ayla,' Lann spoke. 'Take our love with you, forever.'

The cold wind swooped down from the heavy, dirty clouds and took pieces of them away like loose leaves on an autumn oak, and then they were gone.

Shocked and tearful, the four friends held each other for a long time. Ayla was inconsolable at the loss of her beloved uncles, and wailed at the fact that she couldn't say good-bye. It was a good many hours before they began to feel the huge surge of grief subsiding a little. Finny held Ayla's face, and Sean squeezed Benvy tightly; they allowed them-selves to feel happy just to be together again.

The pain inside their hearts couldn't be doused, but they revelled in each other, checking for injuries and marvelling at the fact that they were alive and physically unharmed. They told one another their long stories, gasp-ing at the dangers they had faced. The only thing Ayla's friends left out for now was Taig's betrayal.

'We won't forget them,' Benvy said, and the others agreed solemnly.

'Now we just have to find our way home,' Sean observed. 'How the hell are we going to do that? Can we open the gates like they did?'

It was the first time they had thought about it.

'I think I have the power to do that now,' Ayla said. 'But ...'

'Thank God!' Benvy said. 'It's going to be a long trek, but I can't wait to get home!'

'Agreed!' said Sean. 'I am going to eat the entire house, and sleep for six months!'

Their spirits were up, and the long journey back seemed achievable now that they had Ayla back.

But Finny was not smiling. He was looking at Ayla, concerned. 'Ayla? What's wrong?'

'We have to go back.'

The other two stopped chattering.

'Well duh! That's what we're talking about!' Benvy laughed, puzzled.

'Ayla?' Finny asked again.

'No. Not back home,' she said.

The storm overhead was building. The wind threw out stiff gusts, while thunder drummed in threat.

'Back in there.' She was pointing to the foot of the wilted tree.

Sean and Benvy laughed.

'Yeah, right!' they said, nervously.

'Ayla, what *are* you talking about?' Finny demanded. The sky rumbled.

'Those things: the creatures. I know what they are,' she

said. 'They were girls, just like me. They were taken in the hope that they *were* me. And they were cursed to live down there as those monsters. You saw it. I was nearly one myself.'

Finny, Sean and Benvy just stared at her.

'We are going to save them.' She turned and kneeled at the stump.

'I feel ... different,' Ayla continued. 'Something happened when they healed me: they gave me something. Something *more*. I think I can *do* things. I think I can open these gates!'

She let out a long low hum, and ran a finger in a circle on the stones. The ground cracked open. She turned to beckon them in.

'Come on!' she shouted over the tempest, now wild around them. A fork of lightning lashed at the earth nearby.

The three looked at each other, and then at their friend.

'Wait! Ayla, your eyes!' Benvy shouted.

'What?' Ayla asked.

'They're ...' Sean started.

Ayla's eyes were burning with pure white light. Fronds of electricity flicked from their edges.

'Let's go,' she said, and disappeared through the hole, back into the darkness.